Suddenly a phone rang.

"*Chronicle,*" Wanda said, answering the phone on her desk.

Wanda listened for a moment. Then, with some alarm, she said, "No, I didn't know that."

All eyes in the room had turned toward Wanda. Even Wishbone seemed curious about the conversation.

Wanda's eyes opened wide with shock. "Oh, my gracious. This is awful. Thank you so much for letting me know."

Wanda hung up the phone and rushed over to the railing.

"Folks, it appears there is a breaking story! A big one! A crime story!"

"What is it?" Joe said, eager to know.

Wanda made a wild gesture. "Harold has been stolen!"

WISHBONE™ ***Mysteries***
titles in Large-Print Editions:

#1	*The Treasure of Skeleton Reef*
#2	*The Haunted Clubhouse*
#3	*Riddle of the Wayward Books*
#4	*Tale of the Missing Mascot*
#5	*The Stolen Trophy*
#6	*The Maltese Dog*
#7	*Drive-In of Doom*
#8	*Key to the Golden Dog*
#9	*Case of the On-Line Alien*
#10	*The Disappearing Dinosaurs*
#11	*Lights! Camera! Action Dog!*
#12	*Forgotten Heroes*
#13	*Case of the Unsolved Case*
#14	*Disoriented Express*
#15	*Stage Invader*
#16	*The Sirian Conspiracy*
#17	*Case of the Impounded Hounds*
#18	*Phantom of the Video Store*
#19	*Case of the Cyber-Hacker*
#20	*Case of the Breaking Story*

by Alexander Steele

WISHBONE™ created by Rick Duffield

Gareth Stevens Publishing
A WORLD ALMANAC EDUCATION GROUP COMPANY

This book is a work of fiction. The characters, incidents, and dialogues are products of the author's imagination and are not to be construed as real. Any resemblance to actual events or persons, living or dead, is entirely coincidental.

For a free color catalog describing Gareth Stevens' list of high-quality books and multimedia programs, call 1-800-542-2595 (USA) or 1-800-461-9120 (Canada). Gareth Stevens Publishing's Fax: (414) 332-3567.

Library of Congress Cataloging-in-Publication Data available upon request from publisher. Fax: (414) 332-3567 for the attention of the Publishing Records Department.

ISBN 0-8368-2703-1

This edition first published in 2000 by
Gareth Stevens Publishing
A World Almanac Education Group Company
330 West Olive Street, Suite 100
Milwaukee, Wisconsin 53212 USA

Edited by Kevin Ryan
Copy edited by Jonathon Brodman
Continuity editing by Grace Gantt
Cover concept and design by Lyle Miller
Interior illustrations by Lyle Miller
Wishbone photograph by Carol Kaelson

Printed in the United States of America

1 2 3 4 5 6 7 8 9 04 03 02 01 00

To Barbara Arnold and the many other dedicated folks who keep the nation's small-town newspapers running

FROM THE BIG RED CHAIR . . .

Oh . . . hi! Wishbone here. You caught me right in the middle of some of my favorite things—books. Let me welcome you to the WISHBONE Mysteries. In each story, I help my human friends solve a puzzling mystery. In ***CASE OF THE BREAKING STORY***, Joe, Sam, David, and I step in to help Wanda Gilmore with *The Oakdale Chronicle* when the entire staff calls in sick with the flu. But can my pals and I solve a late-breaking story before the printer's deadline?

The story takes place in the fall, during the same time period as the events that are featured in the second season of my WISHBONE television show. In this story, Joe is fifteen, and he and his friends are in the ninth grade. Like me, they are always ready for adventure . . . and a good mystery.

You're in for a real treat, so pull up a chair, grab a snack, and sink your teeth into ***CASE OF THE THE BREAKING STORY!***

Chapter One

SATURDAY, 9:00 A.M.

"I just love newspapers," Wishbone said with a wag of his tail. "They offer readers so many wonderful stories to chew on."

The white-with-brown-and-black-spots Jack Russell terrier lay stretched out comfortably on the office floor at *The Oakdale Chronicle*. The *Chronicle* was the local newspaper in Wishbone's hometown of Oakdale. And a very noble newspaper it was.

The dog was there with his three best friends—Joe Talbot, Samantha Kepler, and David Barnes. The kids were planning to spend the day learning about . . . well, a typical day in the life of a newspaper. Their assignment was part of a school project for their ninth-grade class at Oakdale High School. Though Wishbone wasn't a student at the school, he figured he had better go along to lend a paw . . . or two . . . or three . . . or four.

"I got hooked on newspapers at an early age," Wishbone told his friends. "Back in my puppy days, I spent quite a lot of time on newspapers."

For some reason, no one seemed to hear him.

Why is it that no one ever listens to the dog? Wishbone thought with frustration. *I'm filled with fascinating information, but sometimes no one seems to listen!*

Wishbone looked around the office, which he had visited many times. The main floor was a spacious area, with brick walls, a high ceiling, and all sorts of interesting-looking equipment. The office had a modern look, but a few old-time wooden filing cabinets lent the place an atmosphere of the historical past.

Most of the staff worked at wooden desks placed around the main floor. Since the staff had not yet arrived, Joe, Sam, and David each sat in a swivel chair at a desk.

A staircase led to a lower level. It had once been the archive area, but now it contained a kitchenette and a darkroom for developing photographs. A level down from there was a basement. That had a general storage space and the archives, or newspaper "morgue." The morgue was a file area that held copies of every issue of *The Oakdale Chronicle* going back nearly seventy years.

"Hello, everyone," Wanda Gilmore called out as she climbed down a staircase that connected her upper-level office to the main floor.

Slender and sharp-featured, Wanda was a lively woman who had all sorts of interests. The way she dressed was typical of her colorful personality. Today she was wearing a checked skirt, a lime-green sweater, and a beret.

Wanda owned *The Oakdale Chronicle,* which she had inherited from her father many years ago. Unlike some newspaper owners, Wanda liked to be involved in the paper's day-to-day management. She worked closely with the staff on the many aspects of the newspaper.

"The rest of the staff should start trickling in soon," Wanda said, taking a seat on an artist's swivel chair. "In the meantime, I've prepared a brief lecture for you kids about the history of newspapers."

"I'm all ears," Wishbone said, raising his ears high.

Joe, Sam, and David turned in their chairs to face Wanda. They all knew Wanda well and enjoyed spending time with her.

After clearing her throat, Wanda began her lecture. "Nowadays information is everywhere. It's on the Internet, TV, radio, newspapers, magazines, and so forth. But back in earlier centuries, it was a real challenge to get information and news out to the general

public. Sometimes it was just passed by word of mouth. And sometimes announcements were made by local officials known as town criers. In a way, they were the first news reporters."

Wanda paused, giving the kids a questioning look.

"Now, do you know any other methods that were used a long time ago to spread information?"

Joe spoke first. "In ancient Greece and Rome, messengers carried the really big news. Often they had to travel for several hundred miles. If the message was really urgent, they even had to run part of the way. I guess they were the track stars of their day."

Joe was an all-around great guy with straight brown hair and a winning smile. He was a dedicated athlete, especially when it came to basketball. Wishbone lived with Joe, and he considered the boy the very best of his best friends.

Then David spoke. "I know my ancestors in Africa sent news from one village to another by beating drums. And the Native Americans used to send news by using smoke signals."

David had curly hair and dark eyes that never missed a trick. He was a whiz with computers and anything else of a scientific or mechanical nature.

Finally, Samantha—known as Sam by her friends—spoke. "In the Middle Ages, minstrels roamed the countryside singing ballads. Those songs told stories about current and historical events."

Sam's hazel eyes were set off by her silky blond hair. She was kind to everyone and talented at all sorts of things in the artistic field.

"Yes, you're all correct," Wanda said, adjusting her

beret. "Here's something else to keep in mind. In the later part of the Middle Ages, as more of the common people learned to read and write, handwritten pamphlets were printed and given out to the public in small amounts. These pamphlets contained news about some really big event, like Columbus's discovery of the New World. Then, shortly after, the printing press was . . . Oh, excuse me."

A telephone was ringing.

Wanda rolled her chair over to one of the office's many phones. She punched a button with a blinking red light, picked up the receiver, and said, "*Chronicle*."

Wanda spoke to the caller for a few moments. Finally, she hung up, showing a worried expression.

"That was the managing editor," Wanda told the kids. "She woke up this morning with a fever, aches, and a sore throat. She's pretty sure she has the flu, which means she won't be coming in to work today. I guess I'll be filling in for her. Well, I've done it before. Now, where was I?"

"The printing press," Joe said.

"Of course," Wanda said, continuing with her lecture. "The printing press, the printing press . . . Yes, well, the printing press was a truly amazing invention. Suddenly, with that machine, it was possible to print many copies of a single document. This paved the way for the first newspapers. They began to appear all across Europe in the early seventeenth century. And then . . . Oh, excuse me."

Again the phone was ringing.

Shortly after Wanda answered the call, another one came in. Wanda signaled for Joe to take it. Then two more calls came. Sam and David answered those.

Wishbone noticed the phones were showing as many red lights as there were on a busy street.

Everyone watched as Wanda talked to the callers, juggling the phone lines one by one.

"Yikes!" Wanda said after finishing the last of the calls. "Four out of five members of the Saturday staff have come down with the flu. I knew there was a bug going around, but I didn't realize it was this bad. They all said they could come in to work if they really had to, but I'd prefer it if they stayed home and got their rest. Well, at least my layout person hasn't called in sick."

The phone rang once more.

"I'll bet ten doggie biscuits that it's the layout person," Wishbone remarked.

No one took the bet. It turned out that Wishbone was right. The layout person had also called to say he was laid up by the flu.

After finishing the call, Wanda let out a heavy sigh.

"What are you going to do, Miss Gilmore?" David asked. "Skip a day of publishing the paper?"

"Skip a day!" Wanda exclaimed with horror. "Never! It's my duty to publish this paper for the citizens of Oakdale every single day of the year—no matter what!"

"Miss Gilmore," Joe said sympathetically, "the three of us will do anything we can to help. I'm just sorry we're not professional newspaper people."

"Hmm . . ." Wanda said, looking at the kids in a curious way. "Maybe you kids *could* be newspaper people—at least for the day."

"Well, I like to write," Sam said, trying to be helpful. "And, of course, photography is one of my hobbies."

"I'm pretty good with computers," David said. "But my writing skills aren't that great."

"Same here," Joe said with a chuckle. "I got a C-plus on my last English paper. That's about as far as you can get from being a professional."

"Actually," Wishbone added, "an F would be further."

Sam smiled at David and Joe. "Hey, don't forget, a few years back, you two guys put together a pretty decent sports newsletter."

Wanda tapped her pen on the desk in front of her, thinking.

"If nothing else," she said, slowly forming her thoughts, "this would be a great learning experience for you three. Certainly better than my interrupted lecture. Besides, I think it might be possible. Today is Saturday. That means we'll be working on Sunday's paper. And the special Sunday sections were already finished yesterday. So all we need to put together today is the main section, and that doesn't have to be more than eight pages. Half of that is ads."

"Miss Gilmore," Joe said with disbelief, "you don't really think that—"

"Fiddlesticks!" Wanda said, tossing her pen into the air. "Of course it's possible! Joe, Sam, David, today you will be the complete staff of *The Oakdale Chronicle*!"

"Yippeee!" Wishbone cried, running around excitedly in a circle. Then he stopped, realizing something.

Hey, she didn't mention me. Well, Wanda's under a lot of pressure. I'm sure she meant that I would be a part of this staff effort. Come to think of it, I believe I've got a bit of newshound *in my bloodline.*

Chapter Two

9:25 A.M.

Wishbone's ears twitched with eagerness. "Okay, folks, let's get to work on our newspaper!"

The dog sat perched in a chair beside Wanda's desk, which was long enough to double as a conference table. The rest of the group—Joe, Sam, David, and Wanda—also sat in chairs around the desk. Everybody was in Wanda's office, which overlooked the main floor. The area was decorated with potted plants and some award plaques that the newspaper had won over the years.

Wishbone examined his fellow staff members. They looked calm enough, but the dog's super-sensitive nose detected scents of nervousness coming from each of them, including Wanda.

I hope the five of us haven't bitten off more than we can chew, Wishbone thought. *It's one thing to read or sit on a newspaper. But it's another matter completely to put one together.*

Becoming very businesslike, Wanda began the meeting. "Every morning at ten, the staff gathers here to discuss what story they are working on for the next day's paper. Since today's staff is composed of three ninth-graders who have never worked for a newspaper, I've decided to hold the meeting a little earlier. We may need the extra time."

"You can say that again!" Wishbone remarked.

"Today I'll be the managing editor," Wanda continued. "My job will be to oversee everything. I will also do the proofreading, work on the ads, and write my gardening column."

"So what do we do?" Joe asked.

"Yeah, what do we do?" Wishbone echoed.

Wanda pointed a pen at Joe. "Today, Joe, you will be the sports editor. I would like you to write about the junior-varsity high-school basketball game that was played last night. I won't give you any other assignments right now. I want to keep you on standby to cover the day's breaking story, whatever that may be."

"'Breaking story'?" Joe asked.

"That means a hot news item that's right in the middle of happening," Wanda explained. "Often it's an unexpected event. But remember, this is just small, quiet, peaceful Oakdale. Most days there is no breaking story. All the same, we need to be prepared."

"I'll do my best," Joe said with a serious nod. "I just hope my best is good enough."

Wanda pointed a pen at Sam. "Sam, you'll be the day's art director. That means you'll be in charge of shooting and selecting photographs for the news stories and adding artwork to some of the advertisements. I also want you to write about today's special town council meeting, which starts at eleven. And if you end up with any spare time, you can do a photographic essay of your own choice."

"Spare time?" Sam said jokingly. "It sounds as if I've got a month's worth of work."

"Just do your best." Wanda pointed a pen at David. "David, you're the computer expert, so you'll be in charge of all the layout work, which involves placing the photos, articles, and ads on each page. You can learn the basics of what you need to know by calling the layout man at home. I'd also like you to interview the high-school custodian to talk about the new union contract. Here's his home phone number."

"Okay," David said, taking a piece of paper from Wanda.

"And if you have time," Wanda told David, "perhaps you could do a review of some new computer game."

"Now you're talking!" David said, displaying a wide smile.

"Hey! What about me?" Wishbone asked, scratching a paw on the table.

For some reason, Wanda didn't respond to Wishbone's question.

Fine, ignore me, Wishbone thought, a bit annoyed. *I'll just create my own assignments. I've always had a nose for sniffing out a good news story.*

"Now, let's see what's on the wire service," Wanda said, sliding her chair over to a computer. "A wire service collects news stories from all over the world. By paying a fee, my paper is allowed to use stories that come in on the wire. We also put some of our own stories on the wire. David, come over and try your hand at accessing the wire service."

David, Joe, and Sam gathered around the computer. Wishbone watched, eager to join the action.

As Wanda gave instructions, David tapped keys expertly on the keyboard. Soon information appeared on the computer screen.

"The *Chronicle* features mostly local stories," Wanda said, her eyes scanning the screen. "But sometimes we print interesting or fun items that we find on the wire service. David, bring up that story—the one with the headline 'Canine Catches Bank Robbers.'"

David tapped a key, and a story appeared. The kids had a good laugh over the story. It was about a dog in Wisconsin that had stopped some bank robbers from making their getaway. The dog sank its teeth into the crooks' money bags and kept pulling on them because it thought they had cheddar cheese inside.

"There's an old expression in the newspaper biz," Wanda told the group. "'Dog bites man' is not a news story, because it happens all the time. But 'man bites

dog' *is* a story. I think 'Canine Catches Bank Robbers' would qualify as a good story. Perhaps we'll place this on an inside page."

"Inside page!" Wishbone exclaimed. "Come on, Wanda, this is a front-pager for sure! And while we're on the subject of cheese, what do you keep to snack on around this place?"

As Wanda and the kids scanned other stories on the wire service, Wishbone got a brilliant idea.

You know what this paper has always been missing? A daily Canine Column. I think I'll start one this very morning. Yes, that'll be my assignment!

Wishbone gave himself a thoughtful paw scratch.

Let's see, what are some subjects I could cover? Oh . . . so many possibilities. Tips for successful food begging. The most popular trees in town. Bone-burial notices. A campaign to improve conditions at the local pound.

Suddenly, Wanda stood and clapped her hands. "Now, listen up, everyone. The paper must be ready to go to the presses by six-thirty sharp this evening. Time is everything. This isn't like a book report for school, when you can tell the teacher you need an extra day. Newspaper folks live by the deadline. On that note, let's get busy!"

Joe, David, and Sam stood up, each seeming overwhelmed by their assignments.

"I can see we'll be working our tails off today!" Wishbone said.

10:00 A.M.

Joe stared at a blank computer screen. The screen was so blank that he felt as if it could swallow him alive.

He was seated at a desk on the main floor of the *Chronicle* office. The desk, which belonged to one of the regular reporters, was cluttered with papers, pens, reference books, takeout menus, and empty coffee cups.

The office was noisier than before. Wanda had turned on a television set that was tuned to a twenty-four-hour news channel. Across the room, a little black box gave off a never-ending crackle of static. It was a police scanner, tuned to the radio channel used for communication by the Oakdale police.

Well, here I am, Joe thought, still staring at the blank screen. *A genuine newspaper reporter for the day. And I'm all set to write a great article about a great basketball game. Just one slight problem—I can't think of a single sentence.*

Moments before, Wanda had given the kids some advice on how to put together a newspaper article. Among other things, she had said the articles should answer the *who, what, where, when,* and *why* of the subject being written about.

Joe placed his fingers on the keyboard. *Let's go, Talbot. Just start answering those questions. If anyone knows about that game, it's you. After all, you play on the Oakdale team!*

Joe typed in: "The small group that was gathered Friday night for the junior-varsity basketball game between Oakdale High and Glenview High received quite a show."

Joe examined the sentence. He felt it wasn't bad. With pleasant surprise, he realized that this single sentence began to answer the *who, what, when, where,* and *why* of the story.

David burst through the office's front door, waving a plastic-wrapped package in the air. "I bought the game! DoomStar! I can't wait to test it out!"

Joe smiled to himself. Wanda had told David he could review a new computer game of his choice for the paper—if he had the time. But David had talked Wanda into letting him review the game as his first assignment. He had just returned from buying it. David had arranged to interview the high-school custodian by phone a bit later in the morning.

David went to a desk, ripped open the package, and popped the CD-ROM into the computer.

Sam ran up a stairway that led from the lower level to the main floor. She was holding a yellowed newspaper in her hand.

"You guys," Sam called out, "look what I found in the basement. It's a *Chronicle* from the 1930s that tells about how some famous gangsters paid a visit to Oakdale!"

Joe smiled again. Sam's first assignment was to report on the special town council meeting. In preparation, she was supposed to read recent issues of the paper that covered the topic the council would be discussing, the city's recycling program. Obviously, she, too, was getting sidetracked.

Wanda appeared at the railing of her office on the upper level. "Sam, don't forget, you have to be ready for the town council meeting at eleven. And, David, you still have to think up questions for your interview."

Joe glanced at Wishbone, who was on the floor, pawing at a stray pencil. Even the dog looked as if he were busy working on a newspaper story. Joe knew, of course, that wasn't really possible.

Joe raised a hand. "Miss Gilmore, I have a question. I was the one who scored the winning basket in this game I'm writing about. It was a pretty decent play. But I feel funny reporting on it. Do you think it'll seem too much like I'm bragging?"

"As a newspaper reporter," Wanda told Joe, "you have a responsibility to write the truth. As the great statesman Thomas Jefferson once said, 'We are not afraid to follow the truth, wherever it may lead!'"

"Does that mean it's okay to say I scored the winning basket?" Joe asked.

"Yes," Wanda replied.

"Miss Gilmore," Sam said with a sly smile, "did that quote happen to come from your unfinished lecture?"

"Yes, it did," Wanda said, taking a small bow. "In fact, while I have everyone's attention, let me say a few more words from the 'truth' section of my lecture. It's important information."

"We're listening," David said, turning away from the flashing explosions on his computer screen.

"Because newspapers reach so many people," Wanda explained, "they have a lot of power. As a result, newspapers often make government leaders and royalty very nervous. In fact, for the first one hundred and fifty years that newspapers were published, they were all heavily censored. By that, I mean the people who ruled would actually tell the newspapers what they could and could not put in print. Now, do you know when American newspapers first won their freedom to print any and all true facts?"

The kids just shook their heads.

"A lot of progress was made around the time of the American Revolution in the late part of the 1700s. The newspapers in the thirteen original colonies printed stories about their dislike of the way the British government was treating them. This had quite a stirring effect on the American people. Finally, the citizens declared war on the colonial rule of Great Britain, and . . . well, you know the rest."

"Then the independent United States of America was formed," Sam said.

"And the forefathers created the Constitution," David added, "which also contained a section called the Bill of Rights."

Joe finished the thought. "And the First Amendment in the Bill of Rights guarantees freedom of the press."

Wanda held a book in one hand and raised a pen

with her other hand, playfully imitating the pose of the Statue of Liberty. "Remember this, folks. Freedom of the press—the right that newspapers have to print the absolute truth—is one of the greatest treasures in this country. It is something to be cherished and used wisely. Aye, 'tis a noble calling, this newspaper profession. Very well. Carry on, troops!"

Suddenly a phone rang.

"*Chronicle,*" Wanda said, answering the phone on her desk.

Wanda listened for a moment. Then, with some alarm, she said, "No, I didn't know that."

All eyes in the room had turned toward Wanda. Even Wishbone seemed curious about the conversation.

Wanda's eyes opened wide with shock. "Oh, my gracious. This is awful. Thank you so much for letting me know."

Wanda hung up the phone and rushed over to the railing.

"Folks, it appears there is a breaking story! A big one! A crime story!"

"What is it?" Joe said, eager to know.

Wanda made a wild gesture. "Harold has been stolen!"

Chapter Three

10:20 A.M.

With a pounding heart, Joe raced out the front door of the *Chronicle* office. Following close at his heels were Wishbone, Sam, David, and Wanda. The four humans and one dog ran to the other side of the street so they could get a full view of the *Chronicle* building.

It was a two-story brick structure sandwiched between two neighboring buildings. Joe knew the *Chronicle* building was one of the oldest structures in Oakdale. A striped awning covered the front door and large ground-floor windows.

Joe ran his eyes up to the building's roof.

"Oh, no!" he cried out. "Harold is gone!"

Harold was a statue made of black metal, about three feet tall. The statue was that of an old-fashioned town crier ringing a bell, preparing to shout the day's news. Harold had stood on the roof for many years. But today the statue was nowhere in sight.

Joe noticed the others looked as surprised as he did. Even Wishbone tilted his head in confusion.

"When I came to the office this morning," Sam said thoughtfully, "I didn't notice if Harold was up there or not. Did anyone else?"

Everyone admitted they hadn't noticed, either.

Wanda stared at the spot where Harold had stood. "Usually I give Harold a little wave or something when I come to work. But this morning I was in such a hurry, I didn't pay poor Harold any attention."

"Was Harold up there yesterday?" David asked.

"Yes, he was," Wanda said with certainty. "Last night around eleven, I left a meeting of the Oakdale Horticultural Club. I walked right by here and, as always, I saw Harold up there, holding his little bell."

"Then we know," David stated, "that Harold was stolen sometime between eleven last night and around nine this morning."

"Those would be great hours for someone to steal Harold," Sam said. "Most of that time, the downtown area is deserted."

"Maybe we should check with the newspaper carriers," Wanda suggested. "They work in the early hours of the morning. Maybe one of them saw something unusual going on."

Joe rubbed his hands together for warmth. It was a cool, damp day in late March. A hazy gray fog blanketed the area, giving an extra sense of mystery to the moment.

"Let me go take a good look up there," Joe said, heading for the building's door.

Joe quickly went inside and ran up to Wanda's office. There he climbed a ladder and then pushed open a trapdoor. He raised himself up through the trapdoor and stood on the slightly angled roof of the

Chronicle building. He walked to the front of the roof, right to the spot where Harold normally stood.

"See any clues?" David called up from the ground.

Joe knelt down. He saw two strong bolts screwed into a black-metal base.

"The bolts that attached Harold to his base are still in place here," Joe called down. "Someone must have used a wrench to unscrew the bolts. Then the culprit removed the statue and put the bolts back."

"Harold has been up there a long time," David said. "That means the bolts must have been rusted in place. So the culprit, whoever it was, must have been pretty strong to be able to unscrew the bolts."

"Joe, you're too close to the edge of that roof," Wanda called up nervously. "I don't want you to fall and hurt yourself."

Joe gave a quick glance around the roof. He saw nothing else that seemed to be an important clue. He

decided to come down so he wouldn't put any more strain on Wanda's nerves. In a few short minutes, Joe rejoined his friends across the street from the *Chronicle* building.

Sam reviewed the situation. "So we know the thief took Harold sometime between late last night and early this morning. And we know the thief is someone with physical strength. And . . . uh . . . I guess that's all we know."

Wanda took off her beret, almost as if she had lost her best friend. "I'm really upset by this. My father placed Harold on that roof shortly after he took over ownership of the *Chronicle*. Harold has stood on that spot for sixty-six years—through rain, wind, heat, and snow. He's become a symbol of the proud tradition of *The Oakdale Chronicle*. I've even grown to think of him as a friend."

Joe knew *The Oakdale Chronicle* had a very interesting history. In 1926 a wealthy fellow named Abel Skelton had bought the building and established *The Oakdale Chronicle*. Six years later, in 1932, Skelton found himself in a poker game with a bold young newcomer to town named Giles Gilmore.

During the game's final hand, the stakes climbed so high that Skelton threw *The Oakdale Chronicle* into the betting. Gilmore won the hand. The following day he took control of the newspaper. Within a few years, he had turned it into one of the finest small-town newspapers in the state. When Giles Gilmore died, he left the paper to his daughter, Wanda.

Joe patted Wanda's shoulder. "Don't worry, Miss Gilmore. We'll find out what happened to Harold."

Wishbone gave Wanda's leg a comforting nudge with his muzzle.

Wanda's expression darkened. "I wonder if Mr. King had anything to do with this."

Joe considered that possibility. Leon King was a shady business tycoon who owned a large portion of Oakdale's land and buildings. The previous year he had tried, unsuccessfully, to take *The Oakdale Chronicle* away from Wanda through some underhanded legal maneuvers.

"Mr. King has proved in the past that he will stop at nothing to make a dollar," Sam pointed out. "But I don't see what he would gain by stealing Harold."

"Maybe King is planning another attempt to take over the *Chronicle*," David guessed. "Maybe he hired someone to steal Harold as a sort of mind game—you know, a way of letting Miss Gilmore know he's going after the paper again. Psychological warfare. It could be just the beginning. He might be trying to scare you into selling the paper."

"Well, let's get back inside the office," Wanda told the group. "It's chilly out here this morning."

As the others went inside, Joe stared up at the building's roof. He figured Harold must have been the victim of foul play. After all, a three-foot statue couldn't just vanish into thin air.

10:40 A.M.

Back inside the *Chronicle* office, Wishbone sat on some scattered newspapers. They were warmer than the floor's bare wood. Joe, Sam, and David took seats at the desks they had been using.

"Should we report this theft to the police?" Sam asked with concern.

Wanda paced back and forth in the newsroom, obviously worried about the loss of Harold. "First thing tomorrow. Today I'm too busy to answer all the questions they'll ask. But, since the theft of Harold has become the day's breaking story, I want Joe to start an investigation. Remember, Joe, I said you would handle the day's breaking story."

"So how do I investigate the story?" Joe asked with a shrug.

Wanda gestured as she paced. "You sort through the evidence, interview people, analyze the facts, then form a conclusion. Investigating a newspaper story is a lot like doing detective work."

Joe leaned back in his chair, a slight smile on his lips. "Detective work, huh? Luckily, I've been reading a bunch of Sherlock Holmes stories lately."

Wishbone, who loved books, sent his tail wagging. "Ah, yes, the greatest detective of all time—Sherlock Holmes. His character was created in 1887 by the famous British author Arthur Conan Doyle. Along with his trusty assistant, Dr. Watson, Sherlock Holmes detected his way through four full-length novels and fifty-six short stories. On top of that, he appeared in countless movies, TV shows, and radio dramas. Aren't you guys impressed that I know all this?"

No one seemed to be listening.

Wishbone gave a sigh. *Just because I'm a dog, they never think I know anything of importance.*

"Oh, I just love Sherlock Holmes," Wanda said,

clutching her hands to her heart. "What story are you reading now, Joe?"

"I started a new one last night," Joe said. "'The Adventure of the Bruce-Partington Plans.' I picked it because my mom told me it featured a newspaper, and I knew I'd be at the newspaper office today."

David turned away from his computer, which showed the bright graphics of DoomStar, the game he had bought to review in his column. "What happens in this one?"

"One foggy morning," Joe explained, "Sherlock is visited in his apartment by his older brother."

"I didn't know Sherlock Holmes had a brother," Sam said, leafing through some recent *Chronicles* she had taken from the basement.

"Of course Sherlock has a brother," Wishbone told Sam. "His name is . . . uh . . . oh, it's on the tip of my tongue. . . . It's . . ."

"The brother's name is Mycroft," Joe said. "He's not as famous as Sherlock, but he's just as smart. He has a high-level position with the British government. Anyway, Mycroft tells Sherlock that the Bruce-Partington plans have been stolen from the government. They are top-secret designs for a new kind of submarine. Mycroft wants Sherlock to find out what's happened to the plans."

"What next?" David asked.

"I don't know yet," Joe answered. "I'm only halfway through the story."

Wanda perched herself on the edge of a desk. The talk of Sherlock Holmes seemed to lift her spirits. "Do you know that Sherlock Holmes is the most popular character in all of literature? I've had a crush on him since I was ten years old. Even though he's not a real person, it sometimes seems like he is."

"Do you really have a crush on him?" Sam asked with a knowing smile.

"Oh, I was fully planning to marry him when I grew up," Wanda declared. "I even sent him a letter telling him so. I knew his address, of course, because it's mentioned in the stories—221–B Baker Street, London, England."

"Didn't Sherlock Holmes stories first appear in newspapers?" Joe mentioned.

"That's right," Wanda replied. "Some of the early ones did. But most of the stories first appeared in a British magazine called *The Strand*. The longer stories would come out in installments, or piece by piece. So you had to keep buying the magazine to see how the story would turn out."

"That's kind of sneaky," David remarked.

"True," Wanda said after a chuckle, "but it also must have been fun. I wish somebody would publish a story like that again. Maybe it's something I could do in my newspaper. I just need to find a mystery writer as talented as Arthur Conan Doyle."

"Good luck," Wishbone said, giving his side a scratch.

"Okay, back to the case of Harold," Wanda said, suddenly all business. "Remember, in the newspaper world, we always have to be aware of the deadline."

"I'd like to pay a visit to Mr. King," Joe said, springing out of his chair. "Maybe by talking to him I can get a sense of whether or not he's the one behind the theft of Harold. And while I'm tracking down the story, I'll try to think of some other suspects."

Wanda stood, watching Joe grab his jacket off a peg on the wall. "Joe, I confess, I'm a little nervous about sending you on this investigation. But I think you'll be all right. I'll tell you the same thing I always tell my regular reporters. Don't do anything dangerous, impolite, or illegal."

"Don't worry," Joe said, putting on his jacket.

Wanda picked up a notepad off a desk and handed it to Joe. "Take this with you."

"Cool," Joe said, examining the small spiral notebook. "A real reporter's pad."

Wanda pulled a cell phone off a shelf and handed it to Joe. "And take this. If you have any questions or problems, give me a call immediately. I'll probably call to check up on you, too. You know the main number here, don't you?"

"I sure do," Joe said, sticking the phone and the notepad into his jacket pockets.

By this point, Wishbone was on all fours, ready for action. "Nothing to fear, Wanda. I'll be leading this investigation, and I won't let anything happen to my faithful assistant, Dr. Watson . . . uh . . . I mean Joe."

"Come on, Wishbone," Joe said, heading for the door. "See ya later, everyone!"

Armed with a pen, the reporter's pad, and the cell phone, Joe and Wishbone left the newspaper office. They were off to investigate their first case as reporters working for *The Oakdale Chronicle*.

Chapter Four

11:05 A.M.

"Watson, the game is afoot!" Wishbone cried out, borrowing a favorite expression from Sherlock Holmes.

Wishbone and Joe moved through the streets of Oakdale's business district. An eerie fog hung over the town, making it seem as if the nearby buildings were covered by a mysterious veil. Wishbone couldn't help but feel that he and Joe were Sherlock Holmes and Dr. Watson, hurrying through the fog-covered streets of old-time London on their newest case.

Soon the boy and dog came to an office building. After riding the elevator to the top floor, they stepped into the elegant reception area of the King Development Corporation.

Wishbone knew all about Mr. Leon King, the owner of the corporation. King was always involved in some sneaky scheme designed to make himself even richer than he already was. A few years back, he had tried to get a permit to build a fast-food restaurant on the edge of Jackson Park. He was unconcerned that such a business would ruin the park's natural beauty. And just one year ago, King had tried to take over *The Oakdale Chronicle* by proving that Wanda Gilmore did not legally own the paper, which she most certainly did.

Wishbone stood beside a couch, so he would not be easily seen. He knew from past experience that dogs were not allowed.

Mr. King may very well be behind the theft of Harold, Wishbone thought. *It would be a perfect way for him to show Wanda he's coming after the paper again. It might be the first step in a campaign to scare her into selling the paper.*

Joe walked over to the receptionist, a stern-looking woman seated at a semicircular desk. "I'd like to speak with Mr. King, please. My name is Joe Talbot. I don't have an appointment, but I'm here for a very important reason."

After a quick glance at Joe, the receptionist said, "I'm certain Mr. King will not be able to see you. He's much too busy."

This lady is King's guard dog. She'll never let us by. I see this situation is going to require some fancy footwork.

Wishbone gave a sharp bark. Then he scampered past the receptionist, running like the wind.

The receptionist sprang to her feet. "Is that a *dog* in this office?"

"No, I'm just a giraffe with a very short neck," Wishbone called as he raced ahead.

"Uh . . . yes, that's my dog," Wishbone heard Joe say. "I'm sorry. I'll get him out of here."

By then, Wishbone had entered a large room where

many well-dressed people were working in cubicles. As Wishbone raced past the desks and different pieces of office equipment, he noticed several people staring at him with amusement. Upon reaching the end of the room, Wishbone put his nose to the ground for a sniff.

Following the scent of Mr. King's cologne, which the dog knew well, Wishbone moved quickly down a hallway, turned left, and entered another hallway. Finally, he stopped near the door of Mr. King's office, which happened to be halfway open. Standing right outside the office, Wishbone eased his muzzle into the doorway for a peek.

Leon King sat behind his desk in a fancy leather chair, talking on the telephone. He was a middle-aged man with a slippery personality. He was dressed in a businessman's suit with a boldly patterned tie, and he wore a sickly sweet cologne.

Just then, Joe hurried down the hallway. He stooped to try to grab hold of Wishbone, but he stopped when he spotted Mr. King. Joe stood outside the office and eased his head into the doorway.

"See, I know what I'm doing," Wishbone whispered. "I got us safely behind enemy lines, didn't I?"

Wishbone raised his ears to hear Mr. King's telephone conversation. Joe listened, too.

"This deal to buy the pharmacy chain," King said, speaking very quietly, "I think it's time to go ahead with it. But listen to me. This has to stay very hush-hush. I don't want anyone getting news of this deal before it's complete. Top-secret, understand?"

Yep, we understand, Wishbone thought. *That's why we're listening.*

"Why?" King spoke into the phone. "Because enemies are everywhere. In the business world, it's dog-eat-dog."

I've never liked that expression.

"I don't think we should talk about this on the phone," King continued. "We need to be careful with e-mail, too. You never know who's poking their nose into your business."

This guy is sneakier than a tree full of cats. And if he's sneaky about the pharmacy deal, he can certainly be sneaky about a newspaper deal.

"Don't worry about it," King continued. "I'll let you know, somehow, when it's time to make the next move. That's it for now. I'll be in touch."

King hung up the phone and leaned back in his chair.

"Which one of us should handle this?" Wishbone asked Joe. "You or me?"

Joe knocked lightly on the door. "Good morning, Mr. King. It's me, Joe Talbot."

Startled, King turned to face Joe. "Who let you in here? How long have you been standing there?"

"I just got here . . . a moment ago," Joe said innocently.

More like a few moments ago, Wishbone thought, keeping out of sight. *But Joe's answer is close enough.*

"Well, you have to leave this very second," King snapped.

"Sir, you'll probably want me to stay," Joe said after a pause.

"And why should I?" King asked, just a little interested.

"Because I'm doing some reporting for *The Oakdale Chronicle,*" Joe mentioned.

"I see," King said with a sneer. "So now Wanda Gilmore is hiring kids to write for her newspaper. I'm not surprised."

"Correction," Wishbone said under his breath. "Kids *and* a dog."

"Miss Gilmore believes everyone in Oakdale is free to have his or her say," Joe said politely. "That includes younger people. Besides, a flu bug has hit the regular newspaper staff."

"What sort of article are you writing?" King asked.

Joe stuck his hands in his jacket pockets. "I'm . . . uh . . . considering doing an article on . . . a few of the town's business leaders. I might call it . . . uh . . . 'The Oakdale Power Brokers.' I figured you would be the best person to start with."

Actually, Joe, you're trying to prove that Mr. King is the one who stole Harold. But why bother the man with the full details? He'd much rather hear the flattery.

A relaxed smile spread across King's face. "Well, I certainly am this town's leading power broker. All right, kid. I'll give you a ten-minute interview."

Joe gave Wishbone a small hand signal, which the dog knew meant "stay." Then Joe stepped into the office, removed his jacket, and sat in a chair across the desk from Mr. King.

Just then, Wishbone heard stern-sounding footsteps approach. Figuring that they belonged to the stern-looking receptionist, Wishbone sneaked into Mr. King's office and took a seat at Joe's feet.

Joe frowned when he saw Wishbone. King was so busy writing that he had no idea the dog was there.

"I'll be quiet," Wishbone whispered to Joe. "I just needed to get away from you-know-who. Maybe she won't think to look for us in here. Okay, let's get this interview rolling."

Joe got his pen and his reporter's notepad ready for action.

11:25 A.M.

Joe looked at Mr. King across the polished surface of the man's desk. Everything in the office looked expensive, including King's haircut and perfectly tailored suit. King leaned back in his big leather chair, seeming very pleased with himself.

This is going to be tricky, Joe thought, his notepad and pen ready to go. *I can't let Mr. King know what I'm really up to.*

Joe glanced at Wishbone, who sat patiently at his

feet. Since King hadn't noticed the dog's presence, Joe decided to let the dog stay put.

"Okay, let's start," Joe told Mr. King. "What exactly do you own, sir?"

"My corporation owns most of the important real estate in the Oakdale area," King explained. "Land and buildings. I've also been increasing my holdings in the media business. So far, I own three television stations and two radio stations. The only thing my media empire does not own is a newspaper. However, in the near future I plan to own one of those, too."

"Which newspaper?" Joe asked, pretending to jot notes.

"*The Oakdale Chronicle*," King replied matter-of-factly.

Joe held his pen in midair. "I don't understand. Wanda Gilmore owns *The Oakdale Chronicle*, and she's never said she wants to sell it."

King ran a finger over the silky surface of his tie. The gesture reminded Joe of a villain twirling his moustache.

"There are ways to encourage someone to sell a business to you," King said. "But, of course, the methods are my concern, not yours."

"So, at some point," Joe said, "you're hoping to force Wanda Gilmore to sell *The Oakdale Chronicle*?"

"*Force* is a strong word. I said *encourage*. And, listen, I'll be doing Wanda a favor. I happen to know the paper isn't making much of a profit these days."

Joe looked hard at Mr. King. "Let me ask you this, Mr. King. Do you ever worry that you might be doing something wrong? I mean, Miss Gilmore cares a lot about that newspaper, and the people of Oakdale like the paper, too. Maybe you should just leave the *Chronicle* the way it is."

"That's what they told Thomas Edison, right before he invented the lightbulb. Or was it the movie projector?"

"What do you mean?"

King leaned forward and placed his arms on his desk. "Wanda Gilmore is living in the past. And she keeps that newspaper in the past, as well. Myself, I've got my eye on the future."

"The future?"

"*The Oakdale Chronicle* covers only small-time local stuff," King explained. "Who cares who won the historical society's annual bakeoff, or if Miss McCafferty's aunt is coming over for afternoon tea? Sure, the paper ought to cover some local news. But today's readers crave a look at the world at large—you know, the big picture. Celebrities, gossip, glitz, scandal. Exciting stuff!"

"But—"

"Besides, the paper's methods of reporting are so boring. The *Chronicle* staff worries over getting every little fact exactly right, even if it means holding back on writing a big story. This is the electronic age. Newspapers need to get the stories out fast, and they can't be afraid to take risks. If they print something that turns out to be inaccurate, well . . . they can always print a correction later."

"I'm not so sure you're right," Joe said. "I think the people of Oakdale like reading about Oakdale. And

I also think the people of Oakdale respect good, honest, fair reporting."

Leaning back in his chair, King laughed.

"What's so funny?" Joe asked.

"I'm getting a lecture on journalism from an eighth-grader."

"Ninth-grader," Joe said, "to be accurate, sir."

"Listen, kid," King said with a wave of his hand, "I'm telling you that paper is living in a bygone era. It's like a dinosaur."

Writing on his pad, Joe said, "It sounds like you're really eager to get hold of the *Chronicle*."

King showed a sneaky smile. "You've got that right, kiddo."

Suddenly, Mr. King shot back in his chair, rolling himself away from his desk in horror.

"What the . . . Something just landed on my shoe!"

Dropping to the floor, Joe saw that Wishbone had crawled to Mr. King's side of the desk.

"I'm . . . uh . . . sorry about this," Joe said, as he pulled Wishbone out from under the man's desk. "I brought my dog in here with me, instead of leaving him outside. I don't—"

"Is Wanda hiring dogs now, too?" King said, checking his shoe. "She can probably get away with paying them even less than kids."

"I'm really sorry," Joe said, scooping Wishbone into his arms.

King stood up angrily. "Try apologizing to my three-hundred-dollar Italian shoes. Look, Joe, I want you and your dog to leave my office—now. This interview is over!"

Immediately, Joe carried Wishbone into the hallway.

"There you are!" the stern receptionist called, her head shooting out of a doorway. "I've been looking all over for you, young man!"

"We were just leaving," Joe said, hurrying away.

As soon as Joe carried Wishbone into the elevator, he set him down. Then he heard the ringing of the cell phone in his jacket pocket. Joe pulled the phone out, pushed a button, and said, "Hello, Miss Gilmore."

But it wasn't Wanda's voice at the other end of the line. It was a deep voice, so deep it was obviously being disguised.

"Listen carefully," the mysterious voice said. "I have information relating to Harold. Meet me in the parking garage by the medical center in ten minutes. I'll be at the back wall."

"Who is—"

The line went dead.

Chapter Five

11:50 A.M.

"Yuck!" Wishbone muttered, his nose assaulted by the sharp odor of car fumes.

He and Joe had just entered a large parking garage located alongside Oakdale's medical center. They had gone there to meet with the unknown person who had called Joe on the cell phone ten minutes earlier.

Only about a dozen cars were parked in the garage, and there were no people around. Wishbone found the semi-dark, concrete world of the garage to be a little spooky. Joe had called the *Chronicle* office to find out if Sam or David could come to act as a backup, but both of them were away.

That's okay, Wishbone thought, as he moved ahead cautiously. *Joe's got me for protection. I'm the roughest, toughest watchdog in town. Dogs like me don't get scared so—Help! What's that?!*

Wishbone's fur bristled. He noticed a figure standing against the back wall, almost blending into the shadows.

The figure wore a long coat, a baseball cap tilted

low over the forehead, and a scarf, which was wrapped around the lower part of the face. It was impossible to recognize who the person was.

"Don't come any closer."

The voice bounced off the concrete walls. It was the same phony-deep voice Wishbone's sensitive ears had heard coming from Joe's cell phone.

Joe stopped where he was, about twenty feet away from the mysterious stranger. The dog tensed his body, ready to flee or defend.

"Who are you?" Joe asked the stranger.

"It is important that my identity remain a secret," the stranger said.

"Okay, it's a secret," Joe said in a brave voice. "What do you know about Harold?"

Wishbone lifted his black nose into the air. *Mixed in with all the fumes, I'm picking up this person's scent. And it's kind of familiar to me. I can't quite place it, though. I'll keep working on it while I listen to the conversation.*

"What is today's date?" the stranger asked Joe.

"March 27," Joe answered.

"And what will the date be in five days?"

"Uh . . . April 1."

"Otherwise known as . . ."

"April Fools' Day."

"What happens on April Fools' Day?"

"Some people play pranks."

"Like who, for example?"

Try as he might, Wishbone could not put a name to the scent his nose was picking up. But the dog had another trick up his fur. Acting very casual, Wishbone wandered slowly toward the stranger wearing the long coat.

Joe made a few guesses. Each time the stranger said no.

After a moment's thought, Joe said, "Well, for the last few years, the captains of the Oakdale High School football team have played some kind of prank on April Fools' Day. Last year, they let loose some gerbils in the school library. The year before, they rolled toilet paper through all the trees on Oak Street."

The stranger nodded his head.

"So what are you saying?" Joe said. "That this year's football captains stole Harold as this April Fools' prank?"

"It's a possibility."

Step by cautious step, Wishbone slowly worked his way closer to the stranger.

"But why would they pull the prank five days *before* April Fools' Day?" Joe asked.

"As the wolf said to Little Red Riding Hood, 'All the better to fool you with.'"

"What's that supposed to mean?"

"You know the Oakdale football team likes to come up with trick plays. This may be their way of throwing everyone off track."

Joe's voice grew braver. "Do you know something about this that you aren't telling me?"

"I am telling you everything I know," the phony-deep voice replied.

By this time, Wishbone was right at the stranger's feet. He grabbed one of the stranger's shoelaces with his teeth and gave a tug, untying the shoe.

Startled, the stranger waved Wishbone away with one hand. Then the person knelt down to retie the shoe. This was what Wishbone had been hoping for. With a lunge, the dog seized the scarf in his teeth, pulling it off the stranger's face.

"Damont!" Joe exclaimed. "I should have known!"

Indeed, the mysterious stranger was none other than Damont Jones, a classmate of Joe's at Oakdale High School. He had the reputation of being the class troublemaker. A smirk was never very far away from Damont's mouth.

Damont grabbed the scarf from Wishbone.

"Okay, Talbot," Damont said, speaking in his normal voice. "Thanks to your little dog, you found out who I am. But, listen, I'm not messing with you here. I'm really trying to help you."

"How did you know to call me?" Joe asked, walking closer.

"A little while ago," Damont explained, "I ran into Sam as she was going into City Hall. She said that you, David, and she were filling in for the regular newspaper staff today. She also told me that Harold had been stolen, and that you were out investigating the crime. So I called Miss Gilmore at the *Chronicle* office and got the number for your cell phone."

"Why so mysterious?" Joe asked, suspicious of Damont's motives.

Damont shrugged. "I wanted to keep my identity a secret because I'm giving you inside information about the captains of the Oakdale High School football team. Have you seen the captains of the football team? They're big. Real big—as in big enough to cause physical injury. And not just on the playing field."

"Yes, they are big," Joe admitted.

"And if you decide to follow up on my tip," Damont said, raising a finger, "you are not free to give out the name of your source. Is that a promise?"

"Yes, I promise," Joe said with a nod.

"Excellent. Later, Talbot."

Damont then wrapped the scarf around the lower part of his face and walked quickly out of the garage.

Wishbone looked up at Joe. "On the one paw, Damont makes a good point. Those football players could be behind the theft of Harold. On the other paw, those football players are big, and they may not like to have us poking our noses into their business. On another paw, as reporters for *The Oakdale Chronicle*, we have a duty to dig up the truth."

Though Joe didn't say anything, Wishbone was pretty sure the boy was following his logic.

"Here's what I think the next item on our agenda ought to be," Wishbone advised. "Lunch!"

Chapter Six

12:05 P.M.

Wishbone turned his muzzle, watching a steaming-hot platter of pizza go by.

The dog sat patiently on the floor of Pepper Pete's Pizza Parlor. He was right beside Joe, who was seated at a table, closely studying the notes on his notepad.

Pepper Pete's had a snazzy decor and incredibly delicious pizza. It was also the only restaurant in town that allowed Wishbone inside with no questions asked. This was due to the fact that the place was owned by Sam's father, a great believer in canine rights.

What was that? Wishbone thought, raising his ears. *I hear something ringing on Joe. Does he have an alarm clock in the pocket of his jacket?*

Joe pulled the cell phone out of his jacket pocket. After pushing a button, Joe said, "Hello, Joe Talbot here."

Oh, yeah. I forgot about the cell phone.

"It's me," Wanda said at the other end of the line. "I just wanted to find out how everything is going."

Wishbone's hearing was so sensitive, he could usually pick up both ends of a telephone conversation. And his nose was sensitive enough to pick up every single pizza scent in the restaurant.

"The investigation is going great," Joe told Wanda enthusiastically. "I've already—"

"Look," Wanda said, sounding rushed. "I don't have time to hear the details right this minute. I just wanted to know that you are all right. And, oh, by the way, someone called the office looking for you. He said his name was Peter Parker. I gave him the number of the cell phone. Did he reach you?"

"Yes," Joe said with a slight smile. "Actually, that was Damont. He was just using the name Peter Parker, which I think is the real name of Spiderman. How are things going at the office?"

"Well enough," Wanda replied. "Sam is still at the town council meeting, and David is working on his assignments."

"Tell Wanda 'hello' for me," Wishbone whispered.

Joe didn't seem to hear.

"Oh, and it seems we have another little mystery around here," Wanda continued. "I received several calls today, all from people living on the two-hundred block of Norman Street. It seems some of the newspapers on this block haven't been delivered for the past few days."

"Did you check with the paper carrier?" Joe asked.

"Yes, I did," Wanda said. "I just called Justin Brown, the boy who delivers papers on that block. He claims that he's delivered the papers on that block every day, and Justin would never lie about such a thing.

Maybe a neighborhood dog is stealing the papers. I don't have time to worry about it today, though."

After a few more words with Wanda, Joe hung up and put the phone back in his jacket pocket.

Wishbone looked up at Joe, frowning. "You know, whenever a crime like this happens, it's always a dog that gets blamed. Why is that?"

Joe returned to studying what he had scrawled on his notepad.

"You're not answering," Wishbone remarked. "That's because you know I'm right."

A waitress came over to take Joe's order.

Wishbone gave his side a thoughtful paw scratch. *Hey, this would be a great story for my Canine Column. I'll solve the mystery myself and save the reputation of all the dogs on the two-hundred block of Norman Street. Unless, of course, one of those dogs really did commit the crime. But I don't think so. Why would a dog steal newspapers? As far as I know, most dogs don't even read!*

The waitress left, having taken Joe's order for a small sausage pizza and a soft drink. Wishbone knew it would take close to eleven minutes and thirty-eight seconds before the pizza would arrive at the table.

"Joe," Wishbone said, rising to his feet, "I'll be back in ten minutes."

Wishbone trotted toward the door. With perfect timing, he was able to exit just as two businessmen entered. Joe had been too busy looking at his notepad to notice.

Ah, yes, Wishbone thought, as he flew on all fours through the business district. *I can feel my blood pumping. I can feel the wheels and gears turning in my brain. I'm off to to solve the Case of the Missing Newspapers. This is a job for Sherlock Hound!*

Wishbone had always felt that he and Sherlock Holmes had a lot in common. They both had sharp senses, brilliant minds, fit bodies, and a deep interest in solving mysteries. True, Wishbone was somewhat shorter than Sherlock, not to mention the fact that he was a dog. But those were small differences.

12:15 P.M.

After traveling a distance, Wishbone reached the two-hundred block of Norman Street. It looked like most of the residential blocks in Oakdale. But today, the grayish fog gave the block a touch of mystery.

Here's the funny thing about fog, Wishbone thought. *Up close, you can't see it all. But then from a distance, you can see it very clearly. I'm sure there's a message in there, but I'm not quite sure what it is.*

Wishbone knew exactly which dogs lived on the block. He spent some time rounding them all up for questioning. It wasn't easy because the dogs didn't seem to understand what Wishbone wanted. But finally he had all the dogs lined up in a row.

There were three dogs present: Lightning, a basset hound; Isis, a Maltese; and Hardy, an English sheepdog.

One of the most impressive things about Sherlock Holmes, Wishbone knew, was his power of observation. The detective could just look a person over and, by picking up tiny details, learn all sorts of things about that person.

For example, on one occasion, a complete stranger came to pay a call at Sherlock's apartment on Baker Street. After a single glance, Sherlock announced to the startled stranger that he was a bachelor, a lawyer, that he suffered from asthma, and that he belonged to a secret club called the Freemasons.

Wishbone decided to try his hand, or paw, at the same trick.

Wishbone walked up to Lightning. The overweight basset hound had drooping eyes, drooping ears, and a wrinkled brow. Though Wishbone respected Lightning's terrific sense of smell, Lightning was the laziest dog Wishbone knew.

"Lightning," Wishbone declared, "you have spent some of the morning sleeping on a carpet with pink, blue, and lavender coloring."

Lightning lifted his nose, just an inch. It seemed he might have been surprised.

"You ask how I know this?" Wishbone continued. "I shall explain. Stuck to your belly are a great number of teeny-tiny fuzz balls of pink, blue, and lavender. This type of fuzz ball, I happen to know, appears only on carpets. Therefore, you have spent the morning napping on just such a carpet."

Lightning didn't move, perhaps from shock.

Wishbone moved on to Isis. The toy-sized Maltese had snow-white fur that had obviously been trimmed and fluffed at a dog salon. A pink ribbon decorated her head. Though she looked like a princess, she had the personality of a wicked queen.

"Isis," Wishbone declared, "you have recently stolen food from a cat's bowl."

Isis showed her tiny fanglike teeth. She might have been offended.

"How do I know this?" Wishbone continued. "There is a strong scent of cat food on your breath. However, it is a well-known fact that no cat will willingly share its food with a dog. Therefore, I conclude that you have stolen the cat food."

Isis gave a yapping bark, as if displeased by something.

"Yap all you wish," Wishbone replied. "Sherlock Hound is always right."

Wishbone moved on to Hardy. The English sheepdog was a good-sized fellow, larger than the others. He had a shaggy coat of gray and white fur, some of which hung over his eyes. The dog looked healthy, rugged, and reliable.

"Hardy, you are new to this town," Wishbone declared. "Indeed, though I have heard of you, we have never met. Nevertheless, I can tell that before you moved to Oakdale, you were actually employed as a sheepdog. By this I mean that you were responsible for herding real, live sheep."

Hardy eyed Wishbone very carefully.

"How do I know this?" Wishbone continued. "Your eyes are far more alert than those of the average household canine. This tells me that you have been trained as a genuine sheepdog."

Wishbone noticed that, for some reason, he was speaking with an English accent. He figured this must be because he was pretending to be Sherlock Holmes.

Wishbone strolled back and forth in front of the three dogs. "Allow me to get to the point. It has come to my attention that someone has been stealing the newspapers on this block. As usual, I fear the blame is about to fall upon one of the neighborhood dogs. That would be one of you three. But worry not. I intend to investigate this matter and see that the true villain is caught."

The three dogs watched Wishbone, saying nothing.

"However," Wishbone continued, "I can't help you unless you are completely honest with me. So if one of you committed the crime, I ask you to confess right here and now. Then I will do what I can to help you get out of the situation as gracefully as possible. I will ask the question only once. Lightning, Isis, Hardy, did any one of you steal those newspapers?"

Wishbone gave the dogs plenty of time to reply. Not one of them uttered a sound.

"Then I shall take the three of you at your word," Wishbone announced. "Or perhaps I should say, the lack of your words. I will assume that none of you three is the newspaper thief. Beginning at once, I shall turn my investigation toward other suspects. I thank the three of you for your cooperation. Good day."

Wishbone walked away slowly, aware that the three dogs were watching him with amazement. Pleased with his performance, Wishbone broke into a run. After all that intellectual work, he was eager to sink his teeth into a well-deserved pizza.

Soon Wishbone entered Pepper Pete's, just as three teenagers left the restaurant. The dog trotted over to Joe. A tray of freshly baked sausage pizza was on the table, two slices already gone.

"Sorry I'm late," Wishbone told Joe. "How about a slice of pizza?"

Joe was busy dialing a number on the cell phone. After a ring, Wishbone heard Wanda answer at the other end.

Joe spoke into the phone. "Miss Gilmore, it's Joe. Could you give me Justin's Brown's address, please?"

"Sure. But why do you need it?" Wanda asked. "As I told you earlier, I already called him about those missing newspapers."

"I want to talk to him about Harold," Joe said. "And I'd prefer to do it in person."

After a moment, Wanda said, "Justin Brown lives at 3255 Temple Lane."

"Thanks," Joe said, before turning off the phone and writing the information on his notepad. Joe looked almost as serious as he did when he was in the middle of a tight game on the basketball court.

"Okay," Wishbone said, pawing at Joe's leg. "Hand over my fair share of the pizza."

Joe set a slice of sausage pizza on an extra plate, which he placed on the floor. Wishbone dug into the pizza as if he hadn't eaten in several weeks.

Wishbone pawed at Joe's leg again. "How about another slice? Watson, did I ever tell you that you are, without question, my best friend?"

Chapter Seven

12:45 P.M.

After finishing their pizza lunch, Joe and Wishbone walked the short distance from Pepper Pete's to Temple Lane.

During lunch, Joe had come up with a new idea for the Harold investigation. There were two things he wanted to do. One, he had to speak with at least one of the *Chronicle's* paper carriers, to see if he or she had seen anything unusual in the early hours that morning. Two, he needed to talk to one of the captains of the high-school football team. Perhaps he could get an idea of whether or not they had stolen Harold as their annual April Fools' prank.

Number two is a delicate situation, Joe thought as he walked. *I'd prefer it if the football player didn't know I'm questioning him about the possible prank. If the players stole Harold, they won't like me knowing about it. And if they didn't steal Harold, they won't like me thinking they did. And, well . . . the captains of the football team are pretty big guys.*

Joe saw a young boy doing some work on his bicycle

in the middle of a front yard. It was twelve-year-old Justin Brown, whom Joe had met a couple of times last year, when they were both in Sequoyah Middle School. He was a thin kid who Joe remembered as being very polite.

Joe had figured that Justin might be able to help him kill two birds with one stone. Not only did Justin deliver papers for *The Oakdale Chronicle,* but he was also the younger brother of Ervin "Grizzly" Brown, one of the football team's captains.

"Hey, Justin, how's it going?" Joe said, as he and Wishbone approached the boy.

"It's going just fine," Justin replied. "What are you doing around here, Joe?"

"I wanted to ask you something," Joe said. "Did you know Harold is missing?"

"Who's Harold?"

"You know, Harold, the statue that stands on the roof of the *Chronicle* building."

"Oh, that Harold. No, I didn't know it was missing. Where did it go?"

Justin quickly turned away from Joe, pulling an oil can from a toolbox. The talk about Harold seemed to make him uncomfortable.

"That's what I'm trying to find out," Joe told the boy casually. "I think Harold was stolen sometime between late last night and early this morning. What time do you get to the *Chronicle* building in the mornings to get your papers?"

Justin squeezed a few drops of oil onto his bike chain. "All of the carriers get there around five. We fold the papers, rubber-band them, and then we set off on our routes."

"Did you notice anything unusual this morning?"

"Like what?" Justin said.

"Well, for example, did you see any strange people hanging around?"

"Nope, I didn't see anyone that early. I never do. Except the other newspaper carriers, of course. But I don't think they'd steal Harold."

Joe heard an animal-like grunting sound coming from Justin's garage. It could have been a bear awakening after its winter hibernation.

"Is that Grizzly in the garage?" Joe asked.

"Yeah. He's working out with his weights."

"He's a great football player. What is he like as a brother?"

Justin accidentally squirted oil on his fingers. "Uh . . . well . . . Grizzly is okay as a brother."

Justin is definitely uncomfortable, Joe thought. *Maybe Grizzly stole Harold, and Justin knows about it. But Justin is probably afraid to say anything because Grizzly is . . . well, pretty big and powerful.*

"Maybe I'll say hi," Joe told Justin.

"Sure," Justin said, wiping the drops of oil off his fingers with a rag.

Joe walked toward the garage. Wishbone followed at his heels. The garage was lit only by the hazy sunlight that came through the opened door. Grizzly Brown lay on his back on a weight bench. A heavily loaded barbell was propped on the iron rest. Obviously, he had just finished lifting a set.

No one would have guessed that Justin and Grizzly were brothers. A junior in high school, Grizzly was five years older than Justin, and probably one hundred fifty pounds heavier. He was a big, beefy, brawny guy with shaggy brown hair and a slightly unshaven face. It wasn't hard to see how he got the nickname "Grizzly."

"Hey, there, Grizzly," Joe said, giving a friendly wave, standing just outside the garage.

"Who are you?" Grizzly grunted, still on his back.

"My name's Joe Talbot. I'm a freshman at Oakdale High. I've watched you play in a bunch of games. You're an awesome middle linebacker. You've got 'college scholarship' written all over you."

"Hope so."

Joe searched for something innocent to say. "You must get pretty bored when it's not football season."

"No kidding," Grizzly said, sitting up to wipe his sweaty face with a towel. "Beats me why they don't

make the football season run all year. Who cares about basketball and baseball and all those other sports?"

"Well, I happen to like basketball. I play junior varsity for—"

Grizzly didn't seem to hear. "And soccer—what's that about, anyway? A bunch of guys with long hair and short pants running around and kicking a funny-looking ball. Who in the world wants to watch that?"

Joe happened to know that soccer was the world's most popular sport, with millions of fans around the globe. But he figured this wasn't the time to argue the point.

Joe casually stepped inside the garage. "Hey, speaking of football, isn't it about time for the captains' annual prank?"

Grizzly stretched one of his muscular arms across his chest. "The prank comes on April 1."

"Do you know what the prank will be this year?" Joe asked, lowering his voice as if he were in on the whole thing.

"Yep."

"What?"

"Not telling." Grizzly grinned mischievously. "Tell you what. There's a hundred seventy pounds on this barbell. I was just using it to warm up. If you can bench-press it one time, I'll tell you about the prank."

Joe had never pressed one hundred seventy pounds, which was more than his full weight. But Joe really wanted to know what had happened to Harold.

"It's a deal," Joe said, taking off his jacket.

12:55 P.M.

Wishbone watched Joe lie on the weight bench, flat on his back.

I know Joe's basketball workouts include weight training, the dog thought with concern. *But one hundred seventy pounds . . . That's almost like lifting a Saint Bernard over your head. Maybe two Saint Bernards.*

"I'll spot you," Grizzly said, moving his big body near the bench press.

Joe got a firm grip on the barbell's handle. He sucked in a deep breath.

"Come on, buddy!" Wishbone whispered with encouragement. "You can do this!"

Releasing a whoosh of breath, Joe slowly pushed the one hundred seventy pound barbell up ward, moving it above his chest. Inch by inch, Joe's straining arms slowly lifted the barbell higher . . . higher . . . higher. . . . Finally, Joe held the weight with his arms fully outstretched, as high as the barbell would go.

Then, with an exhausted groan, Joe lowered the barbell back to its resting spot."Way to go, Joe!" Wishbone cried triumphantly.

"Hmm . . . not bad," Grizzly muttered.

Joe sat up, wearing a satisfied smile. "Okay, Grizzly, I pressed the weight. Now tell me about this year's April Fools' prank."

"No way," Grizzly replied.

"But you said—"

Grizzly laughed, sounding like an evil creature straight out of a monster movie. "I tricked you. I was just pulling your leg."

"You didn't trick me," Joe said angrily. "You *lied* to me."

Grizzly stopped laughing, his expression dead serious. "You're calling me a liar?"

"Watch out!" Wishbone urged Joe. "This guy is bigger than you, me, and two Saint Bernards put together. And you can also throw in a schnauzer."

"Relax," Joe said calmly. "I wasn't calling you a liar. I just . . . Hey, Grizzly, remember that play you made in the last seconds of the Jefferson game? That was awesome."

Ah, good move, Wishbone thought. *When in trouble, change the subject.*

"Oh, yeah, how could I forget?" Grizzly said, a faraway look in his eyes. "We were beating Jefferson by five. . . ."

As Grizzly continued to talk about the game, Wishbone let his eyes roam around the garage. The place contained all the usual garage stuff—tools, paint, cardboard boxes, crates of soft drinks, and household items.

Hmm . . . Let's say, theoretically, that Grizzly and the other football captains stole Harold as their annual prank. Then, theoretically . . . Harold just might be hidden somewhere in this very garage.

Grizzly was still talking. ". . . sure enough, the halfback gets the pitch and . . ."

Right now a circus clown could walk into this garage juggling fireballs, and Grizzly wouldn't notice. Perfect time for me to do some detective work.

Wishbone began to wander around the garage. He was especially interested in investigating the cardboard boxes. He peered inside one box, finding an empty goldfish bowl and containers of fish food. He peered inside another box, finding Christmas decorations.

". . . now the halfback pulls back his arm. He's going to throw a . . ."

Wishbone saw a larger box sitting on top of a stack of suitcases. The box looked just the perfect size for holding Harold prisoner.

". . . receiver catches the ball and goes flying down the field. I'm the only one who can . . ."

Wishbone climbed on top of a pile of automobile tires to bring himself level with the box, which was firmly closed. The dog stretched out a paw and then began to work the box open, all the while listening to Grizzly's play-by-play analysis.

". . . I manage to grab the guy, but he's as slippery as soap. He gets away. Nothing but daylight in front of him. I've got one more chance. I turn up the juice full-throttle. I'm tearing after him and—Hey!"

Wishbone whipped his head around. Grizzly was charging across the garage, straight toward him. All of a sudden, Wishbone understood where Grizzly had gotten his nickname. The guy looked more like a ferocious grizzly bear in the wilds of Wyoming than he did a human being.

Wishbone saw a flash of snarling white teeth, a pair of hairy, meaty arms. Then two giant hands the size of baseball mitts seized the dog around the middle and lifted him high into the air.

"Hey! Careful with my dog!" Joe shouted.

"Yeah, careful with his dog!" Wishbone exclaimed. "That's me!"

Grizzly swung Wishbone around as if he were a football. "This dog was trying to get into that box! And I've got something in there I don't want anyone messing with!"

Joe's eyes shot over to the box. He gave it a curious look. Wishbone figured Joe was thinking the same thing he was thinking. Harold might be in the box!

Very politely, Wishbone said, "Okay, big fella, you can set me down now. Football's not really my sport. I'm more of a stick-chaser."

Grizzly placed the dog gently on the floor. "Look, Joe, I think you and your dog had better get out of here. Both of you are making me nervous. I get that way a lot in the off-season. And when I get nervous, there's only one thing for me to do—pump some serious iron."

Grizzly began to add more weight to his barbell.

"Well, it was good talking with you, Grizzly," Joe said, giving the older boy's shoulder a pat.

Joe signaled for Wishbone to follow him out of the garage. Once outside, Joe waved good-bye to Justin, Grizzly's younger brother, who was still working on his bicycle.

"Sorry I didn't get inside that box," Wishbone told Joe as they walked down the street. "I almost had the touchdown, but not quite. They say the last yard is always the toughest. But I feel certain that Grizzly and the other football captains stole Harold . . . unless, of course, Mr. King did it. One of them must have done it . . . I think. Okay, pal, what's our next play? Joe, are you listening?"

Chapter Eight

2:10 P.M.

The office of *The Oakdale Chronicle* hummed with the energy of mental concentration. Wishbone lay on the floor, his muzzle resting on his front paws. The dog was hard at work, thinking . . . thinking . . . thinking.

The terrier's ears picked up the many noises of a busy newspaper office—the police scanner, the television, the ticking of the clock, Wanda's pen scratching on paper, and fingers clattering over three computer keyboards.

Wanda was up in her office writing her gardening column. Joe was writing his sports article. Sam was writing her town council article. David was writing up his interview with the high-school custodian. Wanda did most of her writing with pen and paper, but the three kids preferred to use computers.

"Hey, everyone," Joe called from his desk. "What's another way of saying 'a player ran down the court really fast'?"

"He charged like a bull," David suggested.

"He streaked like lightning," Sam offered.

Wishbone glanced up. "He galloped on all fours like a prize winning horse on the last lap of the Kentucky Derby."

"Thanks," Joe said, typing in some words. "I think I'll use the lightning image. That's a perfect way to describe this Glenview center."

Myself, I'm getting a little frustrated, Wishbone thought. *I'm running into some real trouble with my Canine Column.*

Wishbone planned for tomorrow's paper to contain the grand debut of the daily Canine Column. For that reason, he wanted to feature something really spectacular—like the solving of the mystery of the missing newspapers. The problem was, Wishbone didn't have the slightest idea who the newspaper thief could be.

Why would someone steal copies of the same newspaper edition? One copy of each edition is just like another. If your picture was in the paper, I could understand. But this thief is stealing the papers day after day.

Wishbone's eyes drifted to the large window at the front of the office. He watched the fog drifting around one of the street's old-fashioned lampposts. A group of about a dozen children walked by pushing grocery carts piled high with newspapers.

Wishbone's tail thumped. *Those kids are pushing grocery carts piled high with newspapers!*

Immediately Wishbone ran to the door. It was open just a crack. He opened it more with his muzzle and trotted outside.

Wishbone stood on the sidewalk, watching the

children with their grocery carts. Recognizing a few of the kids, Wishbone knew this was a group of fourth-graders.

I wonder, Wishbone thought, tilting his head. *Could these kids be running some kind of newspaper-stealing business? I'll question one of them. It's always better to deal with suspects one at a time. I've seen enough cop shows on television to know that.*

Wishbone ran a few steps, then stopped.

Wait. I'd better not let on that I'm investigating the crime of the missing newspapers. I'll need to be more secretive than that. What would Sherlock Holmes do in this situation? . . . Of course! He would use a disguise!

Sherlock Holmes, Wishbone knew, was a master of disguise. Often while investigating a case, the detective would change himself into an entirely different person by the use of costumes, theatrical makeup, wigs, and a little acting talent. While solving some of his cases, he had become a sailor, plumber, horse-keeper, book collector, priest, and even an old lady.

It's not always so easy disguising myself, though. That's because I'm just a little shorter and furrier than the average person. Nevertheless, it can be done. Let's see . . . What can I disguise myself as? . . . Oh, I know. I'll pretend I'm a nine-year-old elementary-school student. Of course, elementary!

Unfortunately, Wishbone didn't have any costumes, makeup, or wigs handy. He would be forced to pull off his disguise through the use of his acting talent alone.

Wishbone hurried after the kids, doing his best to act like a perfectly normal nine-year-old boy. He singled out a girl pushing a cart at the rear of the group.

"Hello, excuse me," Wishbone called to the girl.

The girl kept following her group.

"Hello," Wishbone called again. This time he threw in a bark to make sure he caught the girl's attention.

The girl spun around. Seeing Wishbone, the eyes behind her glasses lit up with pleasure. Her slender figure was topped off by a cute face and brownish-blond hair. She had a tomboy toughness about her, despite her delicate appearance.

"Hi, there, Mr. Doggie," the girl said, kneeling down to Wishbone's level. "My name is Lauren Ostermann. I wonder who you are."

Wishbone trotted over to Lauren. "Oh, no, I'm not a doggie. My name is Walter Wisher. I'm a nine-year-old kid, just like you. You don't know me, of course, because I don't go to your school. I'm visiting from . . . Peoria, Illinois. I'm here in Oakdale for . . . a lunchbox convention. In my hometown, I attend Lassie Elementary School."

The girl looked at the dog curiously. Wishbone realized he had made a serious mistake.

"Uh . . . no, sorry," Wishbone said, correcting himself. "I meant to say . . . Thomas Jefferson Elementary School."

The girl continued looking curiously at the dog. Either she wasn't understanding Wishbone's words, or, more likely, she wasn't believing them.

"What I say is absolutely true," Wishbone insisted. "My name is Walter Wisher, and I'm in fourth grade at Thomas Jefferson Elementary School. My teacher's name is . . . uh . . . Dolly Madison. My favorite subjects are literature, philosophy, and trigonometry."

Wishbone realized he had slipped up again.

"No, wait, sorry," Wishbone said. "I meant to say my favorite courses are reading, arithmetic, and . . . uh . . . gym. Well, really my favorite course is lunch."

Lauren gave the dog's head a few pats. "You sure are cute, but I'd better get back with my group now."

Not wanting the girl to leave, Wishbone barked.

"I'm sorry," Lauren said, standing up, "but I really need to get back with my group. You see, every weekend my class collects used newspapers from all over town. Then every Monday afternoon, one of the teachers drives the papers to a recycling plant that's about fifteen miles away. Pretty soon, Oakdale might have its own recycling program. But the town council is still working on that."

That's true, Wishbone thought, watching the girl closely. *The town council is considering a recycling program. That's what they were discussing at the meeting Sam attended this morning. Still, Lauren is not telling me where she and her classmates are getting their used papers.*

"Are you sure you're telling the truth?" Wishbone said, glancing at Lauren's cart of newspapers.

Lauren pulled half a candy bar out of her pocket.

"I kept this from lunch," Lauren said, unwrapping the candy bar. "It's nutty on the outside, and peanut butter on the inside. Would you like it?"

"Peanut butter, huh?" Wishbone said, licking his chops. "Ah, now you're talking my language. Wait a second. I see what you're doing. *You're trying to bribe me*. But it won't work, little girl. It's not so easy to bribe Walter Wish——"

Lauren held the candy bar near Wishbone's mouth. Before he knew what he was doing, Wishbone had chewed and swallowed the delicious treat.

"Okay, look," Wishbone said with some embarrassment. "Just because I ate the candy bar doesn't mean I'm letting you off the hook. I want the truth, and I want it now."

Lauren placed her hands firmly on her hips. "Mr. Doggie, I really have to go now. It's very important that all those newspapers get recycled. Then we won't have to cut down so many trees, and trees give off carbon dioxide, which creates oxygen, and that's good for the environment."

Hmm . . . the kid sounds as if she really knows what she's talking about.

"Well, maybe you are telling the truth," Wishbone admitted. "Okay, Lauren, you're free to go now. I'm sorry if I caused you any inconvenience. By the way, I'm not really a fourth-grade student at Thomas Jefferson Elementary School. In fact . . . I'm a dog."

"Nice to meet you, Mr. Doggie," Lauren said with a wave.

"Hey, you know what?" Wishbone said. "Today I'm working at the newspaper office. That might be a good place for you to get some more newspapers."

As if she understood, Lauren glanced at the *Chronicle* building.

"Maybe I could get some old newspapers in there," Lauren said to herself. "I'll catch up with the other kids later."

Isn't that what I just said?

2:35 P.M.

Wishbone followed Lauren and her grocery cart inside the *Chronicle* office.

"I brought us a visitor," Wishbone announced to his friends.

Everyone was too busy to hear him.

David went up the steps leading to Wanda's office, carrying a sheet of paper. "Here you go, Miss Gilmore. My interview with the custodian is all done. Now I just need to do some more work on my DoomStar review."

"Thank you, kind sir," Wanda said, as David set the paper on her desk. "I look forward to reading this."

"Miss Gilmore," Joe called from his desk. "I should be done with this sports article in about twenty minutes. And can somebody remind me of the difference between 'who' and 'whom'? I can never remember that."

"Oh, just pick the one you like best," Wishbone advised. "That's what I usually do."

"'Who' refers to the subject of a sentence," Sam said, staring with concentration at her computer screen. "'Whom' refers to a direct object. At least I think that's right."

"That's right," David said, as he returned to his desk. "You say 'Who sent the letter?' or 'The letter was sent by whom?'"

"Well, sure," Wishbone said, as he parked himself on the floor. "If you really want to be picky about it."

"Hi, Miss Gilmore," Lauren called up to Wanda's office.

Wanda looked down at Lauren. "Hi, Lauren." Wanda made introductions. "I haven't seen you in a dog's age. How can I help you?"

"I'm collecting old newspapers for my school's recycling drive," Lauren explained. "Do you have any old newspaper lying around. After all, this is a newspaper office."

"I have some in the basement," Wanda said. "But I don't have time to deal with gathering them up today. My staff is out sick, and I've got a million things to do. Besides, I just realized, we need one more article for tomorrow's paper."

"No, we've got that covered," Sam called up. "Earlier you said it was okay to call Amanda Hollings and ask her if she would write a theater review for the paper. She agreed."

"I remember," Wanda said with a sigh. "But I could really use one more article."

"Maybe Lauren could write an article," David said jokingly.

Sam swiveled her chair to face Lauren. "That's not a bad idea. She could write something from a kid's viewpoint."

"Me, you, and Joe *are* kids," David pointed out.

"And I'm dog," Wishbone added.

"I guess I mean a *younger* kid's viewpoint," Sam said, smiling at Lauren.

"I like that idea," Wanda said, rising from her desk.

"You do?" Lauren asked with surprise.

Wanda eyed Lauren as she came down the staircase. "Lauren, how are your writing skills?"

"Well . . ." Lauren said slowly. "I recently wrote a paper in class. It was about cookies."

"One of my favorite topics," Wishbone said, rising to his feet.

"Tell me about it," Wanda told Lauren.

"Well, the teacher gave each student two cookies," Lauren explained. "And we had write about how the cookies did something to each of our five senses."

"Do you think you could write an article for the newspaper?" Wanda said.

Lauren's eyes twinkled behind her glasses. "Maybe, if it was about sports. I love sports. Especially soccer. I'm the forward on my school's soccer team."

"Joe, you're the sports editor," Wanda said. "What do you think?"

Joe stopped typing and turned to Lauren. "How did your soccer team do this year?"

"Well, the first half of the season we lost every game," Lauren said with a frown.

"Ouch!" Wishbone said.

"But then we switched from Division A to Division B," Lauren said, a smile creeping onto her face. "Then we won every game."

"Hey, there's a great angle for a story," Joe said, snapping his fingers. "A team that went from losing every game to winning every game."

"Lauren could write how it feels to win and how it feels to lose," David put in.

"And she could talk about whether or not winning is the most important part of sports," Sam added.

"Lauren, would you like to try to write an article about your soccer team?" Wanda asked. "I can call the school and explain that I've pulled you away from the recycling drive. I'll also call your parents for permission. If your article turns out well, I'll put it in tomorrow's edition of the newspaper."

Lauren began chewing nervously at a fingernail. "I'm not that great of a writer."

"But will you try?" Wanda asked. "I'm desperate!"

"Sure, I'll give it a try," Lauren said with a shrug.

Putting an arm around Lauren, Wanda escorted her to a vacant desk. "I'll make my calls and you can start your article."

"Kid, you're in the newspaper biz," Wishbone called to Lauren. "If you have any questions, give a whistle."

Wishbone's eyes drifted to Sam's computer. He noticed that she had moved from her town council article to working on the design of some ads. Sam's computer screen showed an advertisement for Beck's Grocery. Big letters proclaimed: "Only a Turkey Would Miss This Sale!" At the moment, Sam was moving a picture of a turkey around the screen with her mouse."

"Miss Gilmore," Sam called out. "Does it matter how big I make this turkey?"

"You can use your judgment," Wanda said, turning on a computer for Lauren. "But make sure you leave enough room to show the sale items. And, Sam, make it look very nice. Beck's is one of our biggest advertisers."

Wishbone settled on the floor to think about his Canine Column. *You know, I'm really getting to like this newspaper business. The energy, the pace, the flow of ideas. Except, you know what? That picture of the turkey is making me mighty hungry!*

Chapter Nine

3:00 P.M.

Deadline, deadline, deadline, Joe thought, glancing at the clock on the wall of the *Chronicle* office. *Our deadline is in exactly three hours and thirty minutes.*

Joe, Sam, David, and Wanda were gathered around the long desk in Wanda's second-level office. As Wishbone had done at the morning's meeting, he jumped up on a chair to join the discussion.

"Wishbone really seems interested in what we're doing," Joe told the others. "Here's a story idea. Instead of 'dog bites man,' how about 'dog works for newspaper'?"

The three kids burst into laughter.

The day was turning out to be a fun experience. Even so, everyone had worked very hard. Wanda had written her gardening column and worked on the paper's advertisements. Sam had written an article about her coverage of the town council meeting, and she had helped Wanda with the artwork for the ads. David had just finished his review of the computer game and written the interview with the high-school custodian.

Since returning to the office about an hour ago, Joe had written his article about the previous night's basketball game. Though Joe knew the article was far from perfect, he felt it was fairly decent.

Maybe I've got some talent for this newspaper business after all, Joe thought, glancing at one of the nearby award plaques. *Sam and David seem to be doing okay, too.*

Joe glanced down at the main floor, where Lauren sat at her desk. She chewed a fingernail as she stared at her computer screen. The nine-year-old girl seemed to be having a tough time writing her article. Joe knew how she felt.

"Hang in there," Joe called down to Lauren. "I'm sure you'll do okay."

Wanda adjusted the angle of her beret, then began the meeting. "At three o'clock every afternoon, the managing editor calls the staff together. At this time, she reviews everyone's progress. Then the decision is made about what is likely to be the day's lead story. That refers to the story that will appear at the top of the front page. "Above the fold," as we in the biz like to say."

"Shouldn't the theft of Harold be the lead story?" David said as he twirled a paper clip.

"Well, that depends," Wanda said in a businesslike tone. "Joe, let's go over your information and see what we have."

Joe had already told everyone a little about the progress of his Harold investigation. But now he went through all his findings in more detail. At times, he looked at his notepad, on which he had scribbled many notes. Everyone listened carefully.

When Joe was finished, Sam rubbed her hands together thoughtfully. "It seems we have two prime suspects as the thief who stole Harold. Suspect number one: Mr. King, who may have hired someone to steal Harold. Motive: to play a mind game with Miss Gilmore in an attempt, once again, to take over the *Chronicle*. Suspect number two: the captains of the high-school football team. Motive: to play an April Fools' prank—even though it's five days before April Fools' Day."

Wanda pointed a pen at Joe. "What is the evidence against Mr. King?"

"We know that if he can't get what he wants legally, he'll try to get it illegally," Joe answered. "And we know he is considering another takeover attempt of the *Chronicle*."

"And remember," David pointed out, "Joe overheard Mr. King discussing a very secret deal involving a pharmacy chain. We can assume he'd be just as secretive with his attempt to take over the newspaper."

"What is the evidence against the football captains?" Wanda asked, again pointing her pen at Joe.

"We know they are expected to pull some kind of local prank on, or at least around, April 1," Joe replied. "And we know Grizzly Brown has something mysterious stashed in a box in his garage, and he doesn't want anyone to know what it is. We also know his younger brother, Justin, seemed nervous when I mentioned Harold."

"And don't forget," David added, "we know that the person or persons who stole Harold must have been strong enough to loosen the rusted bolts on the roof of the building. The football players sure are strong."

"What about Damont Jones?" Wanda asked, stroking her chin with the pen.

Joe nodded. "I've been wondering about Damont myself. He claims he gave me the tip about the football players just to be helpful. That doesn't sound like Damont. I bet he has another reason."

David raised a finger. "Maybe Damont committed the crime. Maybe he gave you the tip just to throw you off track."

Sam stared out a nearby window. "But why would he steal Harold? I suppose he could have stolen Harold just to cause trouble. We all know that 'mischief' is Damont's middle name."

"Well, I guess that pretty well sums up the evidence," Joe said, after taking a final look at his notepad.

A smile broke out across Wanda's face. "Joe, I'd like to congratulate you. Today you have done some excellent investigative reporting."

"Great!" Joe said, feeling his heart leap with pride. "So, do I have enough material to do the lead story?"

"No, you don't," Wanda said.

"I don't?" Joe said, disappointed.

"You have uncovered all sorts of interesting possibilities," Wanda pointed out. "But possibilities are not enough. A responsible newspaper must print facts—hard, cold facts that can't be disputed. This is especially true when people are being accused of wrongdoing."

Joe drummed his fingers on the desk. "It's too bad I can't sneak into Grizzly's garage and take a peek inside that cardboard box."

"But you can't," Wanda said firmly. "That would be illegal, not to mention dangerous."

"This is so frustrating," Joe said, slapping his hand on the desk. "I can just see my story making the front page of tomorrow's newspaper. But we can't put it there!"

"I know. It's a difficult situation," Wanda said with a sympathetic nod. "But this is one of the things that separates a good newspaper from a less-respectable newspaper. A good newspaper holds back on a story until it is certain all the facts are right. The less-respectable newspaper runs a story even if it's not so sure its statements are true."

"So unless I get some really hard facts," Joe said with disappointment, "I guess we don't run a lead story about Harold."

"Correct," Wanda said. "But you can still write a few paragraphs to run at the bottom of the front page. You'll tell who Harold is, say he has been stolen, and urge anyone with information about the theft to come forward."

"Then what will the lead story be?" David asked, twirling his paper clip.

"We can go with Sam's article on the town council meeting," Wanda said, pointing her pen at Sam.

Sam screwed up her face. "That's fine with me. I just hope my story is good enough."

"That's the next order of business," Wanda said, picking up a collection of papers. "I've had a chance to look at the articles you three have written. Now, I'll give you some notes, and then I want you to make the necessary corrections. One more thing. Today, we're all working as professionals, so I'm not going to go easy on my comments."

Joe felt a flutter in his stomach.

Okay, I'm getting nervous again. This is really happening. Sam, David, and I are writing articles that will actually appear in tomorrow's edition of The Oakdale Chronicle. *The articles will be read by tons of people, including practically everyone I know. What if the whole town of Oakdale gives me a failing grade?*

With her professional eyes, Wanda glanced down at the papers she held.

3:15 P.M.

Sitting in his chair, Wishbone scratched a paw on the long desk. "Wanda, I haven't had a chance to write any articles yet, but I'm working on several. Hang tight, please."

This must have been okay with Wanda, because she went right on with the meeting.

Wanda handed a marked-up sheet of paper to Sam. "This is your town council article, Sam. As I've done with all the articles, I've made some written notes on here. In addition, I have comments."

Sam bit her lower lip, looking tense.

"Basically, the article is terrific," Wanda said. "You've made it very clear how all the town council members think about the proposed recycling program."

"But . . ." Sam said, expecting some kind of a problem.

"But," Wanda continued, "you use up too much space on unnecessary details. For example, you've written two entire paragraphs on the design of the City Hall building. Remember, this is a political report, not an architecture column."

"Got it," Sam said, jotting down some notes. "I'll give it a rewrite. Then I should have time for that photo essay you mentioned."

Wanda handed two marked-up sheets to David. "David, your interview of the high-school custodian is most interesting. However, your review of the computer game DoomStar still needs work."

"What's wrong with it, Miss Gilmore?" David asked, nervously unbending the paper clip.

"It seems to be written in a foreign language," Wanda replied. "Here, I'll read an example: 'The one-hundred-twenty-million-pixels-per-sec fill-rate and three-point-five million polygons per sec, combined with the anti-aliasing capability, pack an eye-popping graphic punch.'"

"Huh? What?" Wishbone said, twitching his ears.

"Yeah, I see what you mean," David said with a laugh. "I'll translate all the techno-talk into plain English. Then I should be ready to start work on the paper's layout design."

Joe shifted in his seat, obviously knowing his article would be discussed next.

Wanda handed a marked-up sheet to Joe. "Your sports article, Joe, is in very good shape."

Joe let out a sigh of relief.

"Except," Wanda continued, "I still think you're holding back on the drama of that winning basket you scored. I know you don't want to brag, but remember what Thomas Jefferson said."

Joe repeated the quote. "'We are not afraid to follow the truth, wherever it may lead.' Okay, I'll take Mr. Jefferson's advice and punch up the article. I'll also stay on the breaking story about Harold."

As Wanda made a few more comments, another ninth-grader entered the *Chronicle* building, climbed the stairs to Wanda's office, and took a seat at the long desk. It was Amanda Hollings. She had an overbearing manner, which usually included a lot of dramatic hand gestures.

Sam had come up with the idea of having Amanda write a review of Oakdale High School's spring musical, *My Fair Lady*. Amanda's interest in drama made her the perfect person for the job. With a dramatic movement, Amanda handed Wanda her review, which she had written at home.

As the kids chatted with Amanda, Wanda quickly read over the girl's theater review.

Finally, Wanda looked up from the paper. "The review is very well written, Amanda, but I feel it may be a bit . . . harsh."

"What do you mean?" Amanda asked with surprise.

"I don't want to squash your opinion," Wanda

said, being careful not to offend the girl. "But I feel you're being overly critical about some things, especially in your treatment of the lead actress. Let me explain what I mean."

"I'm not sure I want to hear this," Wishbone whispered to Joe.

Wanda read from the review: "'In the role of Eliza Doolittle, Stephanie Harris did very little, indeed. Her singing was off-key, her acting lacked passion, and her English accent sounded ridiculous. The only thing she excelled at was during the moments when she yelled at the other characters.'"

There was dead silence in the room.

"Ouch!" Wishbone commented. "If we print that review, Stephanie's next role will be in a play called *Who Killed the Drama Critic?*"

Sam, who knew Amanda better than the others, spoke. "Amanda, I know you auditioned for the part of Eliza Doolittle. Instead, you got the role of the maid. I'm sure that was just because you're a freshman. But I

wonder if your disappointment might have influenced your review."

"That's ridiculous!" Amanda snapped with a sweep of her hand. "Stephanie was terrible compared to the actress Audrey Hepburn in the movie version."

"Yes," Wanda pointed out kindly, "but Audrey Hepburn was a professional actress, and Stephanie Harris is just a high-school student. Now, for a high-school student, was she really so bad?"

Amanda looked around, then sounded a loud sigh. "Oh . . . I guess she could have been worse. I'll tone down the review a bit."

"I'd appreciate it," Wanda said, handing Amanda the review. "Okay, let's move on."

Wishbone scratched at the desk for attention. "Hey, Wanda, let me tell you about my Canine Column. I see this as a daily piece about all matters dog-related: tips for successful food begging, the most popular trees in town, bone-burial notices, a campaign to improve conditions at the local pound. That kind of stuff."

Wanda wasn't listening. Instead, she was going over the assignments that each of the kids should be handling next.

"Come on, Wanda, hear me out," Wishbone urged. "We could also get into sports, which dogs are very big on. Cat-chasing, car-chasing, stick-chasing. And one more thing, Wanda. I really think we should put that article about the dog in Wisconsin catching the bank robbers on the front page. I believe—"

Wanda kept talking to the kids.

"Wanda, if you're not going to cooperate with

me," Wishbone said, raising his voice, *"The Oakdale Chronicle* will never boost its canine loyalty!"

"This concludes our meeting," Wanda said, standing up and giving a hand clap. "Off you go, troops. There is work to be done. Our deadline is now just about three hours away!"

Editors can cause so much frustration, Wishbone thought, giving his side an irritated scratch.

Chapter Ten

3:35 P.M.

Joe sat at his cluttered desk in the *Chronicle* office, his chin resting on his folded hands. *I'd really like to solve the mystery of Harold's disappearance today, before the paper's deadlines. Otherwise, we won't be able to run it as tomorrow's lead story. And by tomorrow, a regular member of the staff may be well enough to take over the story.*

The office continued to fill with the noisy activity of a newspaper office. Sam and David were both busy rewriting their articles. Wanda was upstairs in her office, working on the classified ads. Wishbone lay on the floor, chewing on a rolled-up newspaper.

"Miss Gilmore, I finished my article!"

Joe turned to see Lauren standing beside her desk, waving a sheet of paper in the air.

I'm surprised she finished it, Joe thought. *For the past hour she's been doing nothing but chewing her fingernails.*

"Lauren, show it to the sports editor," Wanda called down from her desk.

"That would be me," Joe told Lauren.

Lauren approached Joe and proudly set the paper on his desk.

Joe read the page to himself. It showed only a single paragraph, which Joe read aloud: "'The girls' soccer team at Oakdale Elementary School had a very strange season. At first, they lost every single game. Then they won every single game. Winning was more fun. But sports isn't just about winning.'"

"How is it?" Lauren asked hopefully.

Joe searched for a polite reply. "Well . . . it's a good start. But it's a bit short. Maybe you can . . . fill it out some. You know, add some details."

Lauren chewed a fingernail. "Yeah, I was planning on doing that. But I ran out of things to say."

"You can take another hour or so," Joe said, checking his watch. "Maybe it would help if you interviewed someone. Your soccer coach would be a good choice. She ought to be able to give you some insight about winning and losing."

"That's a great idea!" Lauren said, suddenly clapping her hands. "She's at the elementary school right now. She's in charge of the recycling drive. I'll run right over there!"

Lauren grabbed her sheet of paper and raced for the door.

Smiling at Lauren's enthusiasm, Joe looked at the marked-up copy of his basketball article. *It should not take long to make the revisions on this piece. That means I will have some free time to concentrate on the Harold case. Hmm . . . maybe I can get some help from a real expert.*

Joe unzipped his backpack and pulled out a heavy

book. The volume was fairly old, its binding worn away at the edges. The cover showed the silhouette of a man's face in profile. The man had a hooked nose, and a pipe was clamped between his lips. His coat collar was turned up, and his head was covered by a visored cap known as a "deerstalker."

The book was titled *The Complete Sherlock Holmes*. It contained all fifty-six short stories and four novels that Arthur Conan Doyle had written about the famous detective. Joe had been carrying the book around with him for the past week or so, eagerly reading one story after another.

Like many of Joe's books, this book had belonged to his father. The book was of great value to Joe because his father had died when Joe was only six years old.

Joe opened the book to its bookmarked spot in the middle of "The Adventure of the Bruce-Partington Plans." *Maybe the world's greatest detective will give me some advice or inspiration. Besides, my mom said this story featured a newspaper.*

Joe began to read. In this particular scene, Sherlock Holmes and Dr. Watson were sneaking through the house of a man Sherlock believed to be an international spy. Soon Sherlock found a tin box and pried it open. Inside, he found several newspaper clippings.

The clippings were all of classified ads. Each one contained a mysterious message, such as: "Monday night after nine. Two taps. Only ourselves. Do not be so suspicious. Payment in hard cash when goods delivered. Pierrot."

As Sherlock Holmes realized the importance of the discovery, so did Joe.

"Hey, listen," Joe called out to his friends. "I finally discovered how a newspaper plays a role in this Sherlock Holmes story."

"How?" David called over his shoulder.

"As I told you before," Joe said, "Sherlock is trying to locate the stolen plans for a new type of top-secret submarine. He figures out that one of his suspects, a spy, has been communicating to someone through the classified ads in the *Daily Telegraph*, one of London's biggest newspapers."

"Wouldn't that make it easy for the bad guys to be caught?" Sam said, staring at her computer. "They just announce their plans in public like that?"

"No. They place the messages in a kind of code," Joe explained. "And they don't use their real names."

"Oh, I get it," Sam said.

"Cool," David added.

Joe picked up a newspaper from his desk and turned to the classified ads, which were near the back. "For example," Joe said, putting his finger on one of the classifieds, "this is today's edition of *The Oakdale Chronicle*. One of the classifieds says: 'Please show me a sign of your affection in the coming week. Marty.'"

"Yeah, I get the idea," David said, swiveling his chair to face Joe. "Marty might be the fake name for some master jewel thief. And he's telling a fellow thief that he wants to pull a big heist in the coming week."

Sam also turned her chair to face Joe. "Except I happen to know that classified was placed by Marty Carruthers, who's trying to get Susan Spinella to go steady with him."

"Okay, then let's try another one," Joe said, moving

his finger to a different classified. "This sounds interesting. It says: 'My deed is there, up high, for all to see. Or perhaps I should say not see. Lefty.'"

"Well," David said, staring at the ceiling, "that could mean—"

Sam leaned forward in her chair. "Uh . . . Joe, read that one again, please."

Joe read the message again. "'My deed is there, up high, for all to see. Or perhaps I should say not see. Lefty.'"

The three kids looked at one another, as if all were thinking the same thing.

Sam spoke in a quiet tone. "Whoa! This is creepy. That message sounds like it could be about Harold, doesn't it?"

"It sure does," David said. "You can see the theft of Harold by seeing that Harold is not there to be seen. And 'up high' could certainly refer to the building's roof."

"Hmm . . ." Joe said, leaning closer to the newspaper. "Who is Lefty? I don't know anyone in Oakdale who goes by that name."

"Have you been listening to this, Miss Gilmore?" David called up to Wanda.

"I sure have," Wanda called down. "It just so happens that I have the records for the classifieds right here on my desk. Let me see exactly who placed that ad."

Joe, Sam, and David all looked up at Wanda's office. Even Wishbone was looking in that direction.

Soon Wanda came to the railing that overlooked the main floor. "This is very odd. Apparently an envelope containing that particular classified and a cash payment were slipped through the mail slot early yesterday morning. It was here when the first staff member arrived. But the only name given is 'Lefty.'"

"Wow! That is very interesting," David said in a hushed voice.

"Very, very interesting," Sam agreed.

"Forget 'interesting,'" Joe said, rising to his feet with excitement. "This is incredible! It's exactly like the Sherlock Holmes story! And this means we're on the culprit's trail! Lefty must be the person responsible for stealing Harold!"

Joe sat down, staring at the classified ad. He focused his eyes on the name "Lefty"—printed in little black letters.

"Calm down, everyone," Wanda said, making her way to the main floor. "I'll admit it does sound like Lefty might be the one who stole Harold. But that doesn't make it a fact. We need to analyze this more carefully."

Sam and David rolled their chairs over to Joe's desk. Wanda pulled up a chair, and Wishbone parked himself nearby on the floor.

"We know the where and when," Joe told the group. "Lefty's message was slipped through the *Chronicle's* mail slot early yesterday morning."

"But who is Lefty?" Sam asked. "And who was Lefty sending the message to?"

"And what does the message mean?" David asked.

"And here's the big question," Joe added. "Why would Lefty send a message through the classified section of the newspaper?"

Wanda adjusted her beret, as if doing so would

somehow help her think better. "That is, indeed, a big question. Sending a message through the classified ads makes plenty of sense in the Sherlock Holmes story. Sherlock lived in the Victorian era, during the 1800s. Back then, it wasn't so easy to send messages quickly and privately. The classifieds of a daily paper might have been the best way."

David's alert eyes scanned the office. "But nowadays we've got all kinds of sophisticated ways to communicate: telephone, e-mail, fax. In the electronic age, why would someone choose to communicate about a criminal plan by placing a classified ad in a newspaper?"

The group thought in silence.

David raised a finger. "The classifieds would be a good way to reach a large group of people. Let's say you stole Harold and you wanted to tell these people about it. Using the newspaper saves you the trouble and expense of calling, e-mailing, or faxing everyone in the group. It also saves you the trouble of gathering everyone together."

Joe jumped to his feet. "The captains of the football team! They stole Harold, and they wanted to tell the other members of the team about it!"

"Perhaps," Wanda said, calmly pulling Joe back into his chair.

"Here's another theory," Sam said, tapping the desk with a pen. "Let's say you're nervous about someone finding out about your plan to steal Harold. You're afraid to use the telephone, fax, e-mail, or even be seen meeting in person."

Joe jumped to his feet again. "Mr. King! Those are

some of the things he fears! I heard him say so when he was talking on the phone in his office. He must have hired someone to steal Harold, and he told the person to let him know when the deed was done by using the classifieds!"

"Yes, perhaps," Wanda said, pulling Joe back into his seat. "However, this can't be the work of both Mr. King and the football captains. In fact, it may not be either of them."

"How did Sherlock Holmes handle this situation?" David asked Joe.

"I don't know," Joe said, pulling his book over. "Let me finish the story really quickly."

David and Wanda returned to their desks. Sam ran downstairs to the lower level, where she was developing photographs of the town council meeting in the darkroom. Wishbone stayed right by Joe, pawing at a pencil.

Joe dove back into "The Adventure of the Bruce-Partington Plans." Three pages later, Sherlock Holmes had solved the case, caught the crooks, and returned the submarine plans to the British government. He had also received an emerald tie pin from the queen of England, who was most grateful for Holmes's recovery of the Bruce-Partington plans.

"Hey!" Joe called out, closing his book. "Holmes came up with a brilliant solution!"

In a matter of seconds, Sam and David had rushed over to Joe's desk. Wanda came down from her office. Wishbone looked up at Joe, his pink tongue panting with eagerness.

"What did the master detective do?" Sam asked impatiently.

"Sherlock placed his own classified ad," Joe explained in a rush of words. "But the name he used was 'Pierrot,' which was the code name of one of the bad guys. In the ad, Holmes arranged a meeting at a certain time and place with the other bad guy. The bad guy showed up. And, sure enough, he was the one who had stolen the top-secret plans for the submarine."

"We could do the same thing!" David said excitedly. "We could place a classified ad in tomorrow's paper, telling Lefty he should meet us somewhere at a certain time and place."

"That's what I was thinking," Joe said. "If Lefty sees that we know the name 'Lefty,' he might think we've caught on to his identity. That could make him eager to know exactly who is on to him—enough so that he takes the bait. When he shows up at the arranged time and place, we've nailed our crook."

"It might work," Sam pointed out. "But even if it did, we would have to wait until tomorrow to catch Lefty. That means we won't have the story ready for today's paper."

Joe glanced at the silhouette of Sherlock Holmes that decorated the book's cover. "How about this? We can borrow Holmes's technique, but use a different twist. Instead of putting our message in tomorrow's paper, we can put it on signs. If I put up a bunch of signs around town, there's a decent chance Lefty will see one. We'll set the meeting for . . . let's say . . . five-thirty this evening!"

Joe looked at Wanda, half-expecting she would say no to the plan. However, she seemed as caught up with detection fever as the kids did.

"Brilliant!" Wanda said, clapping Joe on the shoulder. "Joe, you deserve to star in your very own detective story!"

Chapter Eleven

4:20 P.M.

Who stole Harold? Who stole those newspapers? Who stole Harold? Who stole those newspapers?

As Wishbone thought, he walked around in a never-ending circle, following his tail. He was getting dizzy, but he couldn't seem to stop moving.

There was so much mental energy in the *Chronicle* office, the place seemed to vibrate. The closer the deadline time of six-thirty came, Wishbone realized, the more urgent everything seemed to become.

Joe was operating the copy machine, which hummed and sent off flashes of light. The boy had made a sign and was now making copies of it so he could post them around town. The signs were part of his plan to lay a trap for Lefty.

"Miss Gilmore," David called from his desk. "I'm almost done with my rewrite on the DoomStar review. Then I'll be ready to get cracking with the layout of the paper."

"Fine," Wanda called down from her upstairs office. "And I'll get you the number for Bill Patterson, the regular layout guy. He's at home, and he'll tell you everything you need to know about operating the hardware."

"Actually," David pointed out, "you mean software."

Sam was busy loading film into her camera. "Miss Gilmore, I'm going to shoot that photographic essay now. I'm just going to take some pictures of the buildings right here on Oak Street. They look really atmospheric with all this fog. Hopefully, I'll get some good pictures. Then I'll write some captions to go with them."

"Sam," Wanda called down, "the regular photographer said you were welcome to use her digital camera. I know it lets you develop the pictures faster, especially color."

"I think I'd feel more comfortable with my own camera," Sam said, putting some camera supplies in a shoulderbag. "These will be black-and-white, and I should be able to have them developed by the deadline."

"Fine," Wanda called down.

Lauren Ostermann burst through the front door.

"Joe, I'm finished!" Lauren cried, waving a sheet of paper over her head. "My soccer coach helped me add some more stuff to my article. It's still not real long, but it's better than before. I wrote the rest of it in pen because there was no computer handy. Just ignore the cross-outs."

As the copier spat out signs, Joe took the article and examined it.

Wishbone pawed at Lauren's leg. "Hey, Lauren, would you happen to have another candy bar in your pocket?"

Lauren was too busy watching Joe to answer.

After a few moments, Joe said, "Lauren, you did a fantastic job on this story. You've really captured the idea that competition and teamwork are the most important part of playing sports, not just the winning and losing. And you got some great quotes from the coach. I think this story can definitely work in tomorrow's paper."

"Really?" Lauren said.

Joe ran up the steps to Wanda's office, carrying Lauren's article. Wishbone lifted his ears to hear the conversation on the level above.

"Lauren's article is a bit rough," Joe told Wanda. "But I think it's very promising. Just ignore the cross-outs."

"Leave it here, and I'll go over it," Wanda said. "How are the signs coming?"

"They'll be done copying any second," Joe replied. "Then I need to post them around Oak Street. There isn't enough time to go beyond the business district. I'll get Lauren to help out. Hopefully, Lefty will have enough time to see one of the signs. I should be back in around half an hour. That should give me time enough to do the rewrite on my sports article."

After a nod at Joe, Wanda called down to Lauren, "Nice job, Lauren!"

Joe ran down the steps, returning to the copy machine. He took the stack of signs and placed them in his backpack. He pulled two rolls of masking tape from a drawer and threw those in the backpack, too.

Lauren went to the copy machine, chewing a fingernail. "Did Miss Gilmore like my article?"

"She's reading it right now," Joe said, putting on his jacket. "Come on, I need you to help me put up some signs."

"Signs for what?" Lauren asked.

"I'll explain on the way," Joe said, grabbing both his backpack and Lauren's arm. "Let's get moving."

"There sure is a lot of rushing around today," Lauren remarked.

"Welcome to the newspaper business," Joe said, opening the front door.

"Hey, hold that door!" Sam called, heading for the door with her jacket and camera equipment.

"Yeah, hold the door for me, too!" Wishbone cried, also heading for the door. "Wanda, I'll be gone for about half an hour. If you need me, just give a loud whistle."

One after the other, Joe, Lauren, Sam, and Wishbone rushed outside. Too busy for good-byes, everyone headed in their separate directions. Joe and Lauren went south, Sam went north, and Wishbone went west.

4:35 P.M.

I'm headed for the two-hundred block of Norman Street, the dog thought, as he raced past the back of the City Hall building. *At this point, I think the best thing for me to do is revisit the scene of the crime. I'm going to figure out this mystery of the missing newspapers once and for all. I can feel it in my bones. I am going to break the case!*

Like Sherlock Holmes, Wishbone became more alive than ever when he was in pursuit of a criminal. His muscles tightened, his eyes gleamed, and his senses doubled in power. He became like a well-bred hunting hound giving chase to a fox.

When Wishbone reached the two-hundred block of Norman Street, the fog had become a bit thicker. It floated through the air like a layer of smoke. The nearby houses and trees seemed to be phantom shapes, while things in the distance could not be seen at all.

I wonder why it's so foggy today. It's almost as if the spirit of Sherlock Holmes is sending this fog my way. Hmm . . . you never know.

Wishbone saw Hardy, the shaggy English sheepdog, sitting near a porch. A middle-aged man in blue jeans stood beside the dog.

A lady entering the neighboring house waved to the man. "That sure is a fine-looking sheepdog, Kyle. When did you get him?"

"Just a few weeks ago," the man replied, kneeling down to rub Hardy's back. "My brother had a sheep farm out in Utah. Hardy was his sheepdog. Every day he took the sheep to graze and then brought them back to the pen. But my brother just sold his sheep and moved into a little apartment in San Francisco. He thought Hardy would be too big for the place, so he sent the dog out here to me. I'm glad to have him."

Aha! Wishbone thought with great satisfaction. *I was right. Just a few hours ago, I guessed that Hardy had been a practicing sheepdog. That's why they call me Sherlock Hound!*

Hardy's owner went inside his house, leaving Hardy in the front yard. Spotting something with his watchful eyes, the sheepdog trotted over to a garden near the front of the house.

The sheepdog went into a crouch, snarling at a mound of dirt in the garden. The fierceness of Hardy's snarl surprised Wishbone. The sheepdog had seemed to be so gentle.

"Hello, Hardy," Wishbone greeted the sheepdog. "What are you snarling at, pal?"

Hardy glanced at Wishbone, not seeming to know the answer.

"A piece of advice," Wishbone told Hardy. "Never snarl at something until you have formed a theory about what it is. Let me take a look at this mound. I wish I had brought a magnifying glass. Ah, well, my nose is even better."

Wishbone lowered his nose to the mound and sniffed.

Then Wishbone turned to Hardy. "I've determined that whoever is responsible for this mound must have come from deep underground," Wishbone said. "That means . . . yes, that means . . . it must have been a gopher! Grrrrr!"

Wishbone knew gophers were fat, furry, rodent-like creatures that lived underground. They burrowed countless tunnels all over the place—up, down, and sideways. The tunnels allowed them to sneak into gardens, where they feasted on their favorite food, stolen plant roots.

Wishbone didn't like or trust gophers. Their tunnels often interfered with his best bone burial spots. On top of that, a gopher had caused the dog a lot of trouble the year before. The gopher dug holes all over Wanda's yard, and Wishbone had been blamed for the dirty deed.

This particular mound is especially large, Wishbone thought seriously. *It must have been made by the big daddy of all gophers. The Professor Moriarty of gophers!*

A shiver ran through Wishbone's tail.

Professor Moriarty, Wishbone knew, was the archenemy of Sherlock Holmes. Sherlock had once called him "the Napoleon of Crime." The highly intelligent Moriarty ran an underground network of criminals that spread all over London. Moriarty and his gang were responsible for half the evil things that happened in the city, and most of them went undetected.

And I would bet that this big gopher runs an underground network of gophers that runs all over Oakdale. Besides, I have a feeling this gopher may be responsible for the newspaper thefts. I must put my gopher theory to the test. But how?

Wishbone walked back and forth, deep in thought. If there had been a violin handy, he would have played it. Wishbone knew that Sherlock Holmes often played a violin while thinking through a tricky situation.

Finally, Wishbone thought of a plan.

Using his front paws, Wishbone dug at the dirt beside the mound until he had made a small hole. Next he pulled up a flower from the garden, which he placed beside the hole. Then he found a stray piece of newspaper laying in the street. He also placed that beside the hole.

With the trap set, Wishbone hid behind a bush in the garden. Hardy came to hide beside him.

Wishbone and Hardy watched the mound in silence.

Within minutes, a creature's head popped out of the hole. The ratlike thing was covered with bristly fur the color of a peanut. As the creature's full body appeared, Wishbone could see it was bigger and fatter than an overfed cat. It was, in fact, the most gigantic gopher Wishbone had ever set eyes on.

Hardy gave a menacing growl.

"Shh!" Wishbone whispered. "Let's just see what he does. I knew the scent of the flower would draw him to the spot. No doubt he will eat the flower's root. But if he also grabs the newspaper, we'll know this villainous creature is the newspaper thief."

Immediately, the gopher grabbed the flower in its claws. It chewed away greedily at the stringy root. The gopher's two front teeth were long and sharp enough to be deadly weapons.

After finishing with the root, the gopher tossed the rest of the ruined flower away. It glanced around the garden with a pair of black, beady eyes, as if searching for a hidden spy.

"Yes, Professor Moriarty," Wishbone whispered, "it is I, Sherlock Hound. Go on, you dirty, no-good, rodent. Take the newspaper. I dare you. Take it!"

The gopher's eyes fell on the newspaper.

Wishbone held his breath.

Then, as quickly as it had come, the gopher disappeared underground—without so much as touching the newspaper.

"Uh . . . well, maybe I was wrong," Wishbone told Hardy, a bit embarrassed. "It seems this gopher has no interest in newspapers. I tell you, Hardy, this is one of my most baffling cases yet. Well, I'd better get back to the *Chronicle* office. They can't seem to run that newspaper without me. Hardy, my friend, good day."

Hardy peered at Wishbone, his eyes partly covered by fur.

Wishbone headed back to Oak Street, his

thoughts heavy with disappointment. *I fear I won't be able to solve the missing-newspaper case in time to write about it for tomorrow's paper. And now I don't have time to do another article. Oh, well . . . I suppose I'll just have to start the Canine Column another day.*

Wishbone reached the *Chronicle* office just as Sam was carrying her camera equipment back inside.

"Thanks," Wishbone said, following Sam through the door. "Hey, Sam, where are you going?"

Wishbone followed Sam down some steps to the building's lower level. Then he followed Sam inside a small room, figuring it might be a kitchen stocked with tasty snacks. Sam closed the door, leaving the room totally dark.

Oh, I guess this is the darkroom. That would make sense.

Wishbone knew the darkroom was where photographs were developed. The room had to be kept dark most of the time so the film wouldn't be ruined by exposure to too much unnecessary light. Though the dog couldn't see anything, he heard Sam working with her camera, some containers, and some glass bottles. The dog's nose twitched, picking up a funny chemical smell.

After a few moments, Sam switched on a light that bathed the room in a weird reddish glow. She studied some film negatives very closely. Next she did a variety of tasks using the negatives sheets of special paper, and a big machine. After a few minutes, she began soaking the sheets of paper in trays filled with chemical-smelling liquids.

I know that, somehow, all this technical activity is going to turn the film from the camera into real photographs.

Sam reached for a fully developed photograph that she had worked on earlier in the day. It was clipped to a wire with a clothespin. In black-and-white, the picture showed the members of the Oakdale town council seated at a long desk.

After Sam took down the photo, Wishbone followed her back up to the main floor.

"Here's my town council picture," Sam said, setting the photo on David's desk. "Could you scan it into the computer for me? I need to get back to my developing."

"Sure, nice picture," David said, giving the photo a quick glance.

As Sam hurried back downstairs, Wishbone watched David work at his computer. The boy was doing the paper's layout design.

Like a wizard working his magic, David was changing regular-looking text into something that looked like a real newspaper. The articles were being arranged into neat columns filled with small-size newspaper type. David created blank spaces where the headlines and photographs would be inserted.

"Miss Gilmore," David said, as he stopped his work. He looked up toward her office. "Could you tell me what should go where?"

Wanda appeared at the railing of her office. Her beret was crooked, and her face showed the strain of a tough day.

"Give this a try," Wanda instructed David. "Front page: the town council article, the custodian interview, and the brief note about Harold. Page two: the basketball article, Lauren's soccer article, and the stories from the wire service. Page three: the photographic essay on

Oak Street. Page four: the theater review, computer-game review, and the gardening column.

"Great," David said, writing down the information. "And then pages five through eight will contain store ads and the classifieds. And the special Sunday section that was finished yesterday is already at the presses."

"Yes," Wanda said, rubbing her chin, "but what happens if we manage to solve the Harold situation in time to get the story in the paper?"

"It's no problem," David said, as he set down his pencil and worked with his mouse. "We'll cut one of the wire-service stories and then move a few things around."

"Don't cut the dog that caught the bank robbers," Wishbone advised. "And I still think that ought to go on the front page."

Wishbone went to sit by the door. He wanted to wait for Joe, who was still not back from putting up his signs. As Wishbone heard the second hand move by on the clock—tick, tick, tick—he knew the day's final act was drawing ever closer.

I'd better get myself a little rest, the dog thought, half closing his eyes. *At five-thirty we spring the trap on Lefty. Then, oh, yes, the hound will be back on the hunt.*

Chapter Twelve

5:25 P.M.

"The game is afoot!" Wishbone cried. "We're on our way to catch the villainous Lefty!"

In the company of his three best friends, the crime-fighting canine walked alongside the railroad tracks at the edge of town. The sky was just beginning to darken, which made the surrounding fog seem like a gigantic floating ghost. Though not far off, the yellow twinklings of window light in the downtown area seemed to be a hundred miles away.

The group had passed a paper sign taped to a tree. In thick black letters, the sign announced:

LEFTY,
MEET ME AT THE MURPHY HOUSE
AT 5:30 P.M. TODAY!
RIGHTY

"Righty," of course, was Joe.

The kids had been very productive during the past hour. After Lauren and Joe had posted the signs, Joe had finished the rewrite of his sports article. Sam had completed the rewrite of the town council article and prepared her photographic essay. David had finished the rewrite of his DoomStar review and completed most of the layout work.

Wanda was back at the office, going over Sunday's paper with a fine-tooth comb. Lauren had gone home. Though Wanda had been hesitant to let the kids go on their detective mission without any adult supervision, they had convinced her they could handle the situation. Joe brought the cell phone. He had promised Wanda he would call the police if there was any sign of serious danger.

At the moment, the paper was practically all set to be sent to the printing presses. However, if the kids and Wishbone managed to catch the thief who stole Harold in the next fifteen minutes or so, there would be just enough time to write up the story and move it into the lead slot on the front page.

The group moved across a grassy field, nearing their destination.

"Unfortunately, the trap isn't foolproof," Wishbone told his friends. "Lefty might see one of the signs and decide to ignore it. Remember, thieves don't like to be caught. Or, the thief might think that Righty already knows who Lefty is. In that case, Lefty might show up, hoping to persuade Righty not to turn him . . . or her . . . or it in to the cops. It could go either way. Heads or tails. Right or left. Right?"

Soon the group reached the Murphy house, an old, two-story wooden structure. No one had lived there for years. The windows were all boarded up, and the whole place looked as if it could collapse at any moment. Among the local kids, the Murphy house was a popular spot for pranks and having meetings of secret clubs.

"Let's hide," Joe said, leading the way to the bushes surrounding the house. "That way we can see the enemy before the enemy sees us."

Joe, Sam, David, and Wishbone slipped into the bushes. They were well covered by the overgrown branches and leaves.

Several minutes passed by. The time went painfully slow for Wishbone, as slow as the last few minutes leading up to dinnertime every night.

"Look!" Sam whispered finally.

Through the eerie fog, a figure could be seen walking toward the house. It was a big, muscular figure with shaggy hair. Wishbone recognized the person as Grizzly Brown, the middle linebacker of the Oakdale High School football team.

"What do you know!" Joe whispered. "It's Grizzly! He must have been the one who stole Harold."

"Now what do we do?" David asked.

"Maybe we should do nothing," Sam suggested.

"That's not a bad idea," Wishbone agreed. "This guy is big. Very big."

Joe shook his head. "I've worked too hard on this story to let it slip through my fingers. I'm going out there and face him."

Before anyone could stop Joe, he stepped out from the bushes. Wishbone, Sam, and David cautiously followed Joe.

"Hi, there, Grizzly," Joe said with a wave. "Or maybe I should call you Lefty."

Grizzly stopped at the edge of the yard, looking very confused. "Why would you call me Lefty?"

Determination gleamed in Joe's eyes. "You can stop pretending, pal. I know about the April Fools' Day prank."

A storm cloud formed on Grizzly's face. "How do you know about the prank?"

"Never mind," Joe said bravely. "I just know."

Wishbone turned his head, seeing two other figures appear from another direction. He recognized them as the other two captains of the Oakdale High School football team—the quarterback and the center. The quarterback was a fairly large-sized fellow, and the center was even bigger than Grizzly.

Grizzly called to his teammates. "Hey, fellas, this kid tells me he knows all about the prank!"

"How?" the quarterback called.

"Don't know," Grizzly replied.

"Let's find out," the center called.

The three football players began walking steadily toward Wishbone and his friends. Among the three football players, there was so much bulk and muscle that they might have been mistaken for an entire army. The fur on Wishbone's back bristled with fear.

"What do we do?" David whispered. "Stay? Make a run for it? Call for help on the cell phone?"

"They won't hurt us," Sam whispered, looking nervous anyway. "At least I'm pretty sure they won't."

"We'll be fine," Joe told his friends calmly.

Suddenly, Wishbone lifted his black nose into the air.

He was picking up a somewhat familiar scent. It was unmistakably human, but it wasn't coming from the approaching football players or from his nearby friends.

Someone else is in the area. Someone unseen. In my book, one unseen stranger is more dangerous than three very visible football players.

The dog lowered his nose to the ground. He followed the scent's trail, which led him onto the rickety porch of the Murphy house. He gave the front door a good sniff.

The nose is never wrong about these things. Somebody is behind this door. And that's very big news. That means the football players might not be Lefty. In fact, I think there's a very good chance that Lefty is inside the house!

5:45 P.M.

Stay cool, Joe thought, beads of sweat forming on his brow. *You can handle this.*

The three captains of the Oakdale High football team stopped right in front of Joe, David, and Sam. The two groups were facing off, as if they were about to begin the shootout at the O.K. Corral. Joe tensed, suddenly worried about the safety of his friends.

"Relax," said Grizzly Brown, the middle linebacker. "Mulligan, Kabriskie, and I aren't going to hurt anyone. We just want to find out how you know about the prank. We haven't even done it yet!"

This admission surprised Joe. "You haven't done it yet?"

"No," Grizzly insisted. "April Fools' Day is still five days away. Try checking your calendar, kid."

The gigantic center spoke next. "Our prank is to

put a papier-mâché version of the Jefferson High mascot upside down, on the roof of the Murphy house. That's why the three of us are meeting here right now. We want to figure out how we're going to do it."

"Way to go, Kabriskie," the quarterback said, rolling his eyes. "You just gave away the prank!"

"That's all right," Sam said, hiding a smile. "We won't tell anyone."

"So it wasn't the signs that brought these guys here," David said to his friends as he glanced around. "They came to the Murphy house for a totally different reason. That means we're still waiting for Lefty."

Joe stepped forward. "Grizzly, could you tell me one thing? What was in that box in your garage? The one you didn't want my dog getting into."

"Inspirational tapes," Grizzly said, embarrassed. "I listen to them sometimes the day of a game. There, are you happy? I told you one of my strategy secrets."

Joe brushed his hair off his forehead, feeling awkward. "Sorry to have bothered you guys. Looks like I . . . uh . . . got my facts wrong."

The football players made the kids promise not to say anything to anyone about their prank. Then they spent a few minutes checking out the roof of the Murphy house. They tried to figure out how and where they would attach the papier-mâché mascot. Once they had finished their mission, the football captains left.

By that time, no one else had shown up at the Murphy house. Figuring Lefty hadn't swallowed the bait of the signs, Joe decided it was time to give up and leave.

"Arfff!"

Joe turned to see Wishbone standing on the front

porch of the house. Joe signaled for Wishbone to come. But the dog began to paw desperately at the front door.

"Maybe Wishbone senses that someone is inside," Joe told his friends. "Let's take a quick look."

The three kids ran to the porch. After opening the creaky door, Joe led Sam and David inside the abandoned house. The place was dark, damp, dusty, and smelled of mildew. Twilight filtered in through a half-missing board that covered a window.

Joe caught sight of a figure standing in the shadowy light of the hallway. It was a thin boy, neatly dressed. The boy was doing nothing, just leaning against the wall.

It took Joe a moment to realize it was Justin Brown—Grizzly's twelve-year old brother, the paper carrier whom Joe had spoken with earlier in the day.

"Hey, Justin," Joe said with surprise. "What are you doing here?"

"Nothing special," Justin said with his usual politeness. "I just come out here sometimes. It's . . . uh . . . real quiet."

It's quiet, all right, Joe thought. *It's also a pretty spooky place just to hang out in by yourself. It's a lot more likely that Justin came here because he saw one of our signs. That would mean Justin is really . . . No, he couldn't be . . . could he?*

Joe pulled the cell phone from his jacket pocket. "Justin, have you ever seen one of these? Here, check it out."

Joe tossed the phone to Justin. Startled, Justin reached out and caught the phone, leading with his left hand.

"Well, what do you know" Joe said in a low voice. "You're Lefty, aren't you? And you came here because you saw our signs, didn't you?"

Ever so slightly, Justin nodded.

"Are you also the one who stole Harold?" Joe asked.

For a brief moment, Justin looked as if he was considering making a break for it. Instead, he stayed.

"Yes, I stole Harold," Justin said, glancing down at his shoes. "But, listen, Harold is safe. I guarantee it."

A million questions flooded through Joe's mind. Suddenly, Joe realized he needed to answer those questions for his article.

Joe quickly pulled out his notepad and pen. "Justin, my friends and I are working today as reporters for the *Chronicle*. I've spent hours trying to figure out who stole Harold. Now that I've found the culprit—

you—I'm planning to write a story about the theft. Can I interview you about this whole thing?"

After a slight hesitation, Justin said, "Uh . . . yeah . . . I guess it's okay. You can interview me."

Joe stared curiously at Justin. This kid has just confessed to committing a crime, yet he's so calm and polite. Well, I'd better get cracking on this story—fast!

Joe began scribbling at a rapid pace. He was jotting down notes about the events leading up to Lefty's dramatic capture. He didn't want to forget a single detail.

David touched Joe's arm. "No need to rush, buddy. It's almost six o'clock. The paper has to be sent to the presses in thirty minutes. There's no way we can put together a story by then."

"Too bad," Sam said, shaking her head sadly. "I have a feeling this could have been a whopper of a story."

Joe felt his heart sink to the floor. He had worked so hard to solve the mystery of Harold's disappearance in a single day. Unfortunately, the case had been solved just a little too late to beat the deadline for the next day's edition of the newspaper.

Joe looked around, almost hoping to find a solution floating in the air. His eyes suddenly locked on the phone that Justin was still holding.

Seized by an idea, Joe grabbed the phone from Justin and dialed the main number of the *Chronicle* office.

After two rings, Joe heard Wanda say, "*Chronicle.*"

Joe spoke a mile a minute. "Miss Gilmore, it's Joe. Listen, we solved the mystery about who stole Harold. And don't worry, Harold is safe. At least I think he is. I just need a little time to put the story together. Is there any way we can . . . uh . . . you know . . . what is it that newspaper people say . . . yeah . . . 'hold the presses'?"

"I've held the presses a few times," Wanda replied. "But the folks at the printing plant operate on a very tight schedule. We'll still have to send the paper out by seven-fifteen at the latest."

"Great! We can do it!" Joe said, checking his watch. "Call the plant right now and tell them to, 'hold the presses!'"

"Okay. But listen, Joe. Are you sure you have all the facts nailed down?"

"Yes. All the facts are all nailed down. Well . . . no, the nails aren't exactly in place yet, but they will be very soon. We're heading for the office right now. Bye."

Switching off the phone, Joe rushed to the front door of the house. Then he realized he had forgotten something very important—Justin.

"Joe," Justin said, "the reason I stole Harold . . ."

"Wait," Joe said, grabbing Justin by an arm. "Don't say another word until we get to the *Chronicle* office. Come on, everyone, we've got to get busy on tomorrow's lead story!"

Chapter Thirteen

6:07 P.M.

Like a hurricane, Joe, Sam, David, Wishbone, and Justin blew through the front door of the *Chronicle* office. Joe realized he needed to write this story with the kind of speed he used for fast breaks on the basketball court.

"I called the folks who run the presses," Wanda said, hurrying down her office steps. "We have a seven-fifteen deadline. Just over an hour from now."

Joe pointed at Justin, who stood shyly by the door. "Justin, here, stole Harold. We don't know the details yet, but we're about to find out."

"I don't know what's going on," Wanda said, throwing up her hands in confusion. "Suppose I just step aside and let you three do your jobs."

Wanda turned off the TV and police scanner. Then she settled into a chair to watch the proceedings.

Battle stations were taken up. Joe pulled out his pen and notepad. David seated himself at a computer. Sam grabbed a camera from a desktop. Wishbone sat on the floor, careful not to get stepped on. Justin just stood there, not sure what he was supposed to do.

Joe took charge of the situation. "Justin, hold on. Sam, David, first we need an introductory paragraph. I jotted something down on the way back here. Tell me what you think."

"Go ahead," David said, propping his feet on his desk.

"'For the past sixty-six years,'" Joe said, reading from his pad, "'Harold, the statue of a town crier, has stood proudly on the roof of *The Oakdale Chronicle's* building. However, yesterday morning it was discovered that Harold was missing, apparently stolen. The *Chronicle* investigated the matter. Early yesterday evening, the thief was caught.'"

"Great!" Sam said, cleaning the camera's lens.

Joe tore out the page and handed it to David. His fingers flying across the keyboard, David typed in the opening paragraph.

"I can show you where I hid Harold," Justin offered. "He's still on the roof, you know."

"We'd better get some pictures of Harold right away," Sam said, sticking a digital card in the camera. "Thank goodness the regular photographer said I could borrow her digital camera. We'll be able to get these photos right into the computer. How about if we get some shots up on the roof?"

Sam, Wanda, David, and Wishbone rushed out the *Chronicle*'s front door.

Joe took Justin to the ladder that led from Wanda's office to the roof. After climbing, the two boys opened the trapdoor and stepped onto the roof's surface. Justin led Joe to the back of the roof, to an opening where a smokestack had stood many years ago. Justin reached into the dark opening and pulled out Harold.

Harold—the three-foot-high black statue of a town crier ringing a bell—looked no worse for wear. Joe carried the statue, which was fairly heavy, to the front of the roof so the others could see it.

"Harold!" Wanda called out, waving her beret. "Welcome back!"

Joe stood Harold in an upright position. After adjusting the camera's zoom lens, Sam snapped a few shots.

"That should do it," Sam called.

Joe laid Harold on the roof. Then he and Justin climbed back into the office while the others entered through the front door.

Joe picked up his pen and notepad. He was so eager

to capture the story in words that he could feel his body buzzing all over.

Now I understand why people work for newspapers. It's pretty exciting! The regular staff may have gotten the flu bug, but I think that I'm getting the newspaper bug!

Pen poised to write, Joe began pacing the room. "Justin, I'll start by asking: Did you in fact steal Harold?"

"Yes, I did," Justin admitted.

"Please tell me about the theft."

Justin rubbed his hands together, almost as if he were washing them. "Well . . . I had been planning to steal Harold for days. Then, this morning, I did it. The other paper carriers and I get to the *Chronicle* building at five in the morning. But today I showed up earlier. It was dark, and there was no one around. I climbed up the drainpipe, bringing a wrench with me in my jacket pocket. Then I . . . uh . . . loosened the two bolts that attached Harold to the roof."

"That must have been difficult," David said. "Those bolts were probably rusted into place."

"My left arm is very strong," Justin said with a hint of pride. "That's from throwing the papers every morning. And I usually get the papers all the way to the doorstep. Ask my customers. Anyway, I hid Harold."

Looking at his notes, Joe said, "David, take this down, please. 'The thief was Justin Brown, a twelve-year-old paper carrier for *The Oakdale Chronicle*. In the dark hours of Saturday morning, while the town of Oakdale slept, Justin climbed . . .'"

As he paced around the room, Joe put Justin's

story up to that point into article format. David typed as fast as Joe spoke.

"Terrific," Joe said, after completing a few paragraphs. "We've got the *who, what, when,* and *where.* But we don't know the most important fact. Justin, *why* did you steal Harold?"

All eyes in the room, including Wishbone's, stared hard at Justin.

Bashfully, Justin looked at the floor.

"Take your time," Joe said patiently.

"But don't take too much time," David urged. "The paper needs to be at the presses in forty-eight minutes."

Sam went to the water cooler and filled a cup with water, which she brought to Justin. "Here, drink this. Maybe it will help."

"Thanks," Justin said, after gulping the water in one long swallow.

Joe focused his eyes on Justin.

"So . . . why did you do it?"

6:29 P.M.

Joe kept his eyes glued on Justin.

Showing his first sign of real nervousness, Justin sat in a chair. He looked up at a light fixture, as if searching for the proper words. Finally, he spoke.

"I did it because I feel . . . invisible."

"What do you mean?" Joe asked.

"Uh . . . well . . . I'm a pretty average kid, not someone people notice all that much. But it seems like everybody in town knows about my brother, Grizzly Brown, the football star."

Joe sat in a chair near Justin, trying to understand. Everyone else in the room kept quiet, letting Joe handle the interview alone.

"Go on," Joe said.

"Everywhere I go . . . the grocery store, school, the park . . . people stop me and ask about Grizzly. 'Is Grizzly ready for the big game this weekend?' 'How's Grizzly's injured knee?' 'What college do you think Grizzly will play for?'"

"And this makes you feel invisible?"

"Something like that."

"And you feel like the things you do don't get noticed?"

"Uh . . . yeah, I guess that's it. See, the biggest thing I do is work my paper route. It may not be as cool as being a football player. But it's not so easy. Seven days a week I show up here at five in the morning, even when it's rainy or cold. I spend half an hour folding and rubber-banding. Then I ride the route on my bike, throwing papers . . . but . . . well . . . no one sees me."

"Because they're asleep?"

"Yeah, everything is . . . dark . . . empty . . . quiet. Grizzly has hundreds of fans cheering him on. But me—I have no one. By six-thirty, I've finished my route. Then, you know, people walk outside and pick up their papers. I never get any credit . . . no word of thanks or anything."

Joe noticed that Wishbone had crept close to his feet.

"But why did you steal Harold?" Joe asked.

Justin stared at the wall, as if struggling to understand the situation himself. "Hmm . . . well, I think . . . uh . . . I think Harold is sort of like me. No one notices us."

"Go on," Joe urged.

"I figured if I made Harold disappear for just one day, people might notice. They wouldn't notice me. But they would at least notice something I had done. And then I was planning to put Harold back tomorrow morning."

"Tell me about the classified ad from Lefty."

Justin thought for a moment. "Hmm . . . I'm not sure why I did that."

Joe tried to help. "Maybe to advertise what you did?"

"Yeah, I guess so," Justin said, nodding. "It was like a secret way of saying 'Hey, look, everyone. See what I did?' But I used the code name of Lefty because I didn't want anyone to really know that I was the thief. And, uh . . . well, that's the end of my story."

Joe realized that he hadn't written down any of this interview information. But that didn't matter. He hadn't forgotten a single syllable.

"Is there anything else you'd like to say?" Joe asked. "For the record."

Justin spoke quietly. "I didn't mean to cause any trouble. I just . . . I don't know . . . I did something stupid. Miss Gilmore, I'm really sorry. You probably want to call the police and my parents. And you probably don't want me delivering your papers anymore."

Wanda looked at the boy. "Justin, I am not going to call the police and file any charges. But I am going to call your parents and discuss with them a suitable punishment. I am disappointed in you, but I do believe in giving people second chances. You may keep your job."

"Thank you, Miss Gilmore," Justin said. Then he turned to Joe. "Don't you have a story to write?"

After giving Justin a pat on the back, Joe stood. "Okay, folks, back to the article."

Pacing the floor, drawing on a writing talent he never knew he had, Joe began to put Justin's confession into article format. David typed the words. At the same time, Sam studied her computer screen, which displayed all the recently taken photographs of Harold.

In about eleven minutes, the article was finished. Joe, Sam, and David gathered around David's computer to read over the final piece.

"Whoa! This is an intense story," Sam said.

"Yep, it sure is," David added.

Joe nodded, knowing in his bones that the article was great. Yet, for some reason, he didn't feel really proud of it. Suddenly he realized why.

"You know what?" Joe told his friends. "I'm not so sure I want to run this article."

"Why not?" David and Sam said together.

Joe looked at Justin, who was now sitting on the floor, petting Wishbone. "Justin seems like a really nice kid. And if we print this article, it could do some real damage to his reputation. Maybe we should give the guy a break."

"I see your point," Sam said thoughtfully.

"All the same," David said, "I think we have a journalist's duty to run the article. I mean, a newspaper can't decide not to report a crime just because a reporter thinks the criminal is a nice person."

"But this is such a minor crime," Joe argued.

"You didn't think it was a minor crime forty-five minutes ago," David pointed out. "In fact, you had

Miss Gilmore hold the presses because you thought the story was so important."

Wanda watched in silence, letting the kids wrestle with the difficult situation on their own.

Joe stared at the words on the computer screen, realizing they would be read by thousands of people the next morning. At the same time, he heard Thomas Jefferson's words—"We are not afraid to follow the truth, wherever it may lead"—ringing in his head, as loud as the Liberty Bell.

Should I follow my responsibility to write the truth? Joe wondered. *Or should I protect Justin's reputation? I really don't know what is right.*

6:48 P.M.

Wishbone glanced sideways at Justin, who was scratching the dog's neck. *This is a tough call. On the one paw, I'm growing to like this kid. On another paw, he committed a crime. On another paw . . .*

Justin stood up. "Can I say something?"

"Sure," Joe told Justin. "What's on your mind?"

"Believe it or not," Justin said simply, "I think *The Oakdale Chronicle* is a great paper. I read it every day after I finish my route. And, well . . . I'd hate to be the guy who made the paper . . . go against its principles."

"What are you saying?" Joe asked.

Justin took a deep breath, as if making a tough choice. "I stole Harold because I wanted people to notice something I did. At the same time, I don't really want them to know it was me who did it. You know what I mean? If the truth comes out, it'll . . . be kind of embarrassing. And I'm sure my parents will be disappointed in me. But . . . I . . . uh . . . well . . . it's better to tell the truth."

Wishbone tilted his head, watching Justin with shock.

"Wow!" Sam said in a low voice. "This is about the bravest thing I've ever heard of."

"No kidding," David agreed. "The guy insists we print the truth about him, even though the truth makes him look pretty bad."

Suddenly, Wanda looked misty-eyed. "It's like something out of a great novel by Charles Dickens or Victor Hugo or . . . Arthur Conan Doyle."

Joe began pacing the room with growing excitement. "Wait, wait, wait. You know what? This angle will make our lead story even more amazing. Picture it. A baffling crime is committed. The criminal is hunted all over town, no stone left unturned. Finally, the criminal is caught. He gives a full confession, a heartbreaking story of feeling invisible. Then, at the very last moment, the villain becomes a hero!"

"Hmm . . . not bad," Wishbone said.

"That's perfect!" Sam said, clenching a fist in triumph. "We'll write how Justin insisted we run the story. . . . We get to print the truth, and Justin gets credit for his honesty."

"What do you think, Miss Gilmore?" David asked.

Wanda looked at the clock. "I say you've got twenty-two minutes to finish the lead story!"

Immediately, Joe began revising the article. "David, let's start the story with this: 'Yesterday, Justin Brown went from being *The Oakdale Chronicle*'s worst enemy to its best friend. Here is the incredible . . .'"

Seven minutes later, with a little help from Sam and David, Joe's "villain to hero" story was completed. At the top of the article, David typed in the byline "by Joe Talbot."

Wow! Wishbone thought with wonder. *Joe did that so fast I barely had time to make any suggestions.*

Then Wishbone witnessed some lightning-fast computer action.

Wanda went to a computer at one of the desks. Through the office's networking system—zip!—David sent the just-written story from his computer to Wanda's computer.

Wanda read through the story carefully, now and then typing in some editorial adjustments and proofreading corrections.

Meanwhile, Sam's computer showed the color photograph of Harold that she had selected and sized. Zip! Sam sent the photograph over to David's computer.

The second Wanda finished making her corrections—zip!—she sent the story back to David's computer.

Tensely, Wishbone glanced at the clock. To the dog's sensitive ears, every tick sounded like the banging of a hammer.

"Okay, we're in the home stretch," David said, as everyone gathered around his computer.

"Eight minutes left," Joe whispered tensely.

Keeping cool under pressure, David called up the layout of the newspaper. The text was arranged in neat columns, and the pictures were all in place. David moved some elements around, clearing space at the top right of the front page. Then he placed Joe's article there and inserted Sam's photo of Harold alongside it.

"I have to admit," Wanda said with amazement, "computers have made this process a lot easier. Not so long ago, we were pasting the stories onto cardboard by using hot wax. In fact, not so long ago, we were using typewriters. Do you kids even know what a typewriter is?"

"Isn't that what the dinosaurs typed on?" Sam said with a smile.

"The *Chronicle*'s technology may be new," Joe said, smiling at Wanda, "but its principles are as old as the Bill of Rights."

"I feel badly that I don't have anything ready for my Canine Column," Wishbone said, changing the subject. "I should have something by tomorrow . . . Monday at the latest."

After a few more adjustments, David said, "Okay, all we need now is a headline for the lead story."

Joe glanced at the clock. "Come on, staff, we need something really dramatic. And really fast."

"'Harold, Glad to Have You Back!'" David suggested.

"'Harold Hurries Home!'" Sam said enthusiastically.

"'Harold, Harold, Harold!'" Wishbone barked.

Joe looked at Justin, who was watching all the activity with great interest.

"You know," Joe said, rubbing his chin, "it seems like the focus of our story is more about Justin than Harold."

"'Justin Caught Just in Time,'" Sam offered.

"'Justin Sees Justice Done!'" David exclaimed.

"'Wishbone, the Wonder Dog, Saves the Day!'" Wishbone barked.

"I've got it," Joe said, with a hand clap. "'In the End . . . the Paperboy Delivers!'"

Everyone looked at Wanda, who gave a big nod. Justin showed a pleased smile.

At the very top of the lead story, above Joe's byline, David typed: "In the End . . . the Paperboy Delivers!" Then he put the words into big, bold, black headline letters.

"All done," David announced. "Miss Gilmore, can I send the paper to the presses?"

"Yes, you may send it to the presses," Wanda said.

David tapped a few keys. A modem sounded a high-pitched screech that made Wishbone's ears twitch. Finally, David sent the paper from his computer to the printer's presses, which were located a few miles outside town.

"Hallelujah!" Wishbone cried, running around in an excited circle. "We did it! We've completed the Sunday edition of *The Oakdale Chronicle*!"

All the humans collapsed in chairs, everyone looking exhausted. The clock showed seven-fourteen, one minute short of the deadline.

"As we say in the newspaper business," Wanda told the staff, "'the newspaper is put to bed!'"

Chapter Fourteen

SUNDAY, 5:25 A.M.

Wishbone lay in his usual nighttime sleeping spot, at the foot of Joe's bed. But the dog hadn't slept much. The puzzling situation with the missing newspapers echoed in his mind, like voices bouncing off a canyon wall.

Finally, Wishbone sat up. He realized he wouldn't get a decent night's sleep until the problem was completely solved.

The house was still. Wishbone heard no sound except for the steady ticking of the clocks around the house.

"Watson, wake up," Wishbone whispered urgently. "I need to discuss the Case of the Missing Newspapers with you."

Wishbone was really whispering to Joe, who lay fast asleep under the covers. But the dog had become so interested in Sherlock Holmes lately that he could not resist calling Joe "Watson" now and then. Besides, he and Joe were the very best of friends, together through thick and thin, just like Sherlock and Watson.

"Watson, wake . . ."

Wishbone quieted, deciding to let Joe sleep. The boy had been through an exhausting day, working for *The Oakdale Chronicle* and assisting Wishbone with the Case of the Stolen Statue.

Wishbone figured he would solve the case on his own. With a burst of energy, he jumped to the floor and went to the collection of various items that he kept stored under the bed. Finally, the dog found a bone, which he had borrowed from the dinner table two nights earlier.

Taking the bone in his mouth, Wishbone moved to the rug beside the bed. Sherlock Holmes, Wishbone knew, often smoked a pipe while he thought through the details of a difficult case. Indeed, he spoke of extremely puzzling cases as being a "three-pipe problem."

This case with the missing newspapers is a three-bone problem, Wishbone thought as he lay down. *Unfortunately, I have only one bone handy. Nevertheless, I shall find the truth—and I shall find it soon!*

Holding the bone with his front paws, Wishbone attacked it with his teeth.

He also took another cue from Sherlock Holmes. The great detective usually solved his cases by the use of something called "deductive logic." Sherlock often described this type of logic by saying something similar to this: "When you take away all that is impossible, whatever remains, no matter how improbable, must be the truth."

Wishbone let his mind wander back to all the suspects he had come across the previous day. He would subtract the ones who could not possibly have stolen the newspapers and then see if anyone was left.

The gigantic gopher could not have stolen the newspapers, Wishbone reasoned. *The gopher is certainly sneaky enough to commit the crime, as most gophers are. But the gopher would have absolutely no reason for doing so.*

Wishbone shifted position, to get a better grip on the bone.

Lauren and her fourth-grade companions could not have stolen the papers. They would have reason for doing so—the newspaper recycling drive. But those kids are not the least bit criminal by nature.

As he gnawed, Wishbone realized he was thinking with an English accent.

Which brings me back to the three dogs who live on that particular block of Norman Street. Lightning, the basset hound, is far too lazy to bother stealing newspapers.

Wishbone's teeth made a fresh attack on the bone.

Isis, the Maltese, does indeed steal food. But she would never stoop to stealing newspapers. The newspaper print would rub off on her white fur and make a mess.

Wishbone paused with his gnawing.

Which brings me to Hardy, the English sheepdog.

Wishbone rolled the bone over and over in his mouth, chewing it from every possible angle. He was thinking so deeply that both his brain and his teeth began to ache.

About ten minutes later, Wishbone released the bone from his mouth. Suddenly, he knew, without a doubt, who had stolen the newspapers.

The game is afoot!

Wishbone ran from the bedroom, raced down the steps to the first floor, entered the kitchen, and slipped through his personal doggie passageway in the back door.

The morning was still blanketed in nighttime's darkness. The fog from the previous day had cleared, but a prickly mist filled the air, tickling Wishbone's fur. There was not a soul in sight, animal, human, or otherwise.

Wishbone raced like the wind!

5:50 A.M.

In his role as Sherlock Hound, Wishbone reached the two-hundred block of Norman Street.

Wishbone crouched in a front yard, hiding behind a well-trimmed shrub. He ran his eyes up and down the block. The entire neighborhood seemed to be asleep. There was nothing in sight except the unlit houses and the many dancing flickers of mist. The chilly air caused the dog to shiver beneath his fur.

Then a figure appeared at the end of the block. Focusing his eyes, Wishbone could see that it was Justin Brown riding his bicycle. Two big baskets on the rear of the bike were stuffed with the Sunday edition of *The Oakdale Chronicle*.

Riding slowly, Justin pulled newspapers from the baskets and hurled them into the different yards. Wishbone admired how skillfully Justin carried out his paper-carrier job. The boy's left arm was strong and sure, sending the newspapers very close to, and sometimes onto, the front porches.

After a few minutes, Justin finished with the block. Wishbone watched the boy pedal on, disappearing from view.

Wishbone wagged his tail back and forth, waiting eagerly for what he knew would happen next.

In less than a minute, another figure appeared, as if out of nowhere. It was a good-sized dog with shaggy white-and-gray fur. As expected, Wishbone recognized the figure as Hardy, the English sheepdog.

Hardy trotted to a newspaper near a porch and took the paper in his mouth. Then the sheepdog moved on to the next house, where he approached another newspaper. Hardy set the first newspaper down, then managed to grab both newspapers in his mouth. Hardy moved on to the next house, where he added a third newspaper to his mouth.

His mouth fully loaded, Hardy ran to the end of the block. Staying a safe distance back, Wishbone chased after the sheepdog.

Hardy turned the corner and entered an alleyway. It was surrounded on both sides by wooden backyard fences. Following behind, Wishbone saw Hardy take the papers to a spot right near a fence.

Wishbone ducked behind the trash cans of a neighboring house. He kept his eyes fixed on Hardy. The English sheepdog set the three newspapers on the ground. Then he arranged them, almost lovingly, with his paws. By this time, the night's darkness was melting into a hazy gray dawn.

Wishbone noticed that Hardy was adding the three newspapers to a collection of about two dozen older newspapers. The papers were not piled on top of one another. They were laid out, very neatly, side by side.

Leaving his hiding place, Wishbone approached Hardy.

The sheepdog turned his muzzle. He gave a growl

so ferocious it made the fur on Wishbone's tail shoot upward.

Hardy's teeth glistened in the mist.

"The game is finished," Wishbone said calmly. "Hardy, I know that you are the newspaper thief. Similar to a famous expression, 'You are a wolf in a sheepdog's clothing.'"

As he recognized Wishbone, the sheepdog's fierceness eased away. Hardy's expression changed into puzzlement.

"How did I know it was you?" Wishbone said, seeing he was no longer in danger of being attacked. "My dear fellow, it was elementary. A simple use of deductive logic."

Wishbone realized he was once again speaking with an English accent.

"I shall explain what I have deduced," Wishbone said, sitting on the damp ground. "Until recently, you were a sheepdog in the state of Utah. Every day you would escort the sheep to a grassy area, perhaps on a mountainside. The sheep would spend the day eating the grass. For some reason, that is their favorite food. I understand sheep are not the world's most intelligent creatures."

Hardy peered at Wishbone curiously, from under the fur overhanging his eyes.

"While the sheep grazed," Wishbone continued, "you would keep watch over them. You would make sure the sheep didn't stray too far. You also kept a lookout for enemies of the sheep—wolves, coyotes, and other breeds of our more aggressive canine cousin. If one of those creatures approached, you would frighten it away."

Hardy only watched, speaking not a word.

"At the end of the day," Wishbone went on, "it would be your job to gather the sheep together and lead them back to their pen. There they would be safely locked up for the night."

Hardy kept silent, not denying this fact.

Wishbone paused for effect, then continued. "Several weeks ago, however, your owner sold his sheep and sent you to live with his brother here in Oakdale. You were forced into retirement. You no longer had the job of a sheepdog. And yet—*the same habits remained!*"

Hardy stared at Wishbone with a look that might have been astonishment.

"When I first met you yesterday," Wishbone said, after pawing a fly away from his ear, "I noticed the extreme watchfulness in your eyes. And I now understand why you growled at the gopher mound. You imagined that the gopher might be some creature threatening your sheep."

Wishbone glanced at the neat collection of newspapers.

"Which brings us to the stolen newspapers," Wishbone said with special emphasis. "In your mind, you thought of these newspapers as sheep. You knew it wasn't right for the 'sheep' to be scattered about during the dark hours, which is when the papers are delivered. So every morning, you bring the newspapers to this safe spot by the fence."

Hardy glanced at his paws. Wishbone thought he detected a sheepish look in the dog's eyes.

"Hardy," Wishbone said in a more gentle tone, "I

see no need to report you to the authorities. I truly believe that you are a decent dog and that you mean no harm. Indeed, you believe you are doing a good thing. However, my dear fellow, this business of stealing newspapers must stop. You see, humans depend on their newspapers a great deal."

Hardy moved his head slightly. Wishbone thought this might be an understanding nod.

Wishbone lowered his voice to a whisper. "And I'll let you in on a little secret. Very soon, *The Oakdale Chronicle* will begin running a daily Canine Column. That, I'm sure, is something that would interest you."

Hardy looked at Wishbone, perhaps with interest.

"Now listen to me," Wishbone said, looking Hardy square in the eyes. "If you wish to continue with your sheepdog habits, that is understandable. But I recommend you find a different sheep substitute. May I suggest, perhaps . . . garbage."

Wishbone studied Hardy's expression, trying to figure out what the sheepdog was thinking. On the one paw, it seemed that Hardy hadn't really understood a word Wishbone had spoken. On the other paw, it seemed that Hardy understood completely and would never steal another newspaper again. Wishbone chose to believe the second theory.

"Excellent, my dear fellow," Wishbone said, a smile on his black lips. "And, Hardy, I hope you very much enjoy your life here in Oakdale. If you ever need anything, just give a bark."

Wishbone and Hardy spent a few moments giving each other friendly sniffs. Then, after nudging Hardy farewell with his muzzle, Wishbone left the two-hundred block of Norman Street.

As Wishbone headed home, he saw the sun peeking through the distant trees, sending a hint of warmth to his fur. The mist had disappeared. Like a photograph developing, the surrounding world was changing from gray into its true and beautiful colors.

Ah, yes, it looks like a pleasant morning, Wishbone thought, as a delivery truck drove by. *I wonder what Mrs. Hudson will be cooking for breakfast.*

Mrs. Hudson was the housekeeper employed by Sherlock Holmes. In reality, breakfast at the Talbot house was cooked by Joe's mother, Ellen. But Wishbone didn't see any harm in staying inside his imagination a little longer.

After all, given the chance, what dog wouldn't wish to be Sherlock Holmes for a day?

Chapter Fifteen

9:00 A.M.

Wishbone ran his eyes over the Sunday edition of *The Oakdale Chronicle*. He was perched in a chair at the kitchen table in the Talbot house. Joe, Sam, and David were also present, the group having gathered that morning to examine the newspaper together.

To celebrate the occasion, Joe's mother, Ellen, was cooking a breakfast with all the trimmings. The smells of sizzling bacon and toasting bread drifted temptingly to Wishbone's nose.

"It's good most of the regular *Chronicle* staff was well enough to return to work today," Joe said, a little sadly. "All the same . . ."

The previous day seemed like a crazy dream to Wishbone. And yet, *The Oakdale Chronicle* spread out before him was proof in black-and-white, with a few color photographs, that the day had really happened.

Wishbone replayed the day in his mind, including the final episode. After a takeout dinner of Chinese food in the office, Wanda had driven the kids and Wishbone to

the printing plant so they could see the printing stage of the newspaper process.

The plant was a big building a few miles outside town. Most of the small-town newspapers in the area were printed there. The press operators were right in the middle of working on the Oakdale paper when the group arrived.

David had sent the paper to a computer at the plant, which sent the digital images to a machine. This machine turned the images into photographic negatives. The negatives were then put on another machine and shot with blinding flashes of ultraviolet light. This machine burned the images into aluminum plates, each plate the size of a single newspaper page. An aluminum plate was made for every page of the paper.

Then the plates were taken into the printing-press room. The printing press was a gigantic, factorylike machine about as big as a house. The plates were curved and then attached to rollers. After a bell rang, the press roared to noisy life. Things went pumping, spinning, whirring, and jumbo rolls of blank paper shot paper through the press at an amazing speed. The whole setup reminded Wishbone of a carnival ride he had no desire to try.

He did like the ink, though. The press contained trays of different-colored ink—black, yellow, a bluish-green shade called cyan, and a reddish-blue shade called magenta. The black was used for the text, and all four colors were combined in different amounts to produce the color photographs. The four colors were so beautiful that Wishbone was tempted to dip his paws in and do a little paw painting on the floor.

Soon the press was spitting out complete sections of the newspaper, perfectly printed, cut, and folded.

The newspaper sections were taken to another room and put on another machine that had a winding conveyor belt. This machine inserted one section of the paper inside another and then automatically tied the finished newspapers into neat bundles.

The bundles were placed on the floor, where they would be picked up by a truck around four-thirty in the morning. The truck would deliver the papers to the *Chronicle* building, where the paper carriers would be waiting to start their daily routes.

And then the carriers bring the paper right to our houses, Wishbone thought, staring at the newspaper on the kitchen table. *It's a pretty amazing process.*

"Oh, I forgot to tell you all something," Joe mentioned. "I called Damont last night. I wanted to know the real reason he gave me that tip about the football players. At first he claimed he was just trying to help. But then I got him to admit there was a little more to it."

"Like what?" David asked.

Joe grinned. "He thought that it would be funny to see me go after three guys who were big enough to be professional wrestlers."

"Yeah," Sam commented, "that sounds more like our Damont."

After sharing a laugh, the kids spent some more time reading over the articles they had written. By then, Ellen had eggs scrambling in a skillet.

"Just think," Joe said with a disbelieving smile, "all over town people are reading this very same newspaper—the one we put together."

David nodded, his eyes on the paper. "And all over the country—no, make that the world—folks are reading other newspapers with other stories."

"It's such a comforting thing," Sam remarked. "Having the paper right there at your doorstep every single day. I guess it's as much a part of morning as alarm clocks and orange juice."

"You know what I think?" Wishbone said, leaning in to look at the front-page photograph of Harold. "Newspapers are like paper-and-ink versions of Sherlock Holmes. They search through the byways of life, in the cities, towns, and countryside, and then they bring us, the reader, The Truth. Not to mention a little entertainment."

No one seemed to hear these words of wisdom.

"I heard something interesting today," Ellen said, as she dished the scrambled eggs onto plates. "While I was out taking my morning walk, I ran into Mrs. Hernandez. She told me there was a serious electrical problem at the movie theater. They had to cancel the movies last night, and they may have to do the same thing today."

After a pause, David said, "Wow! That's a pretty important story. I hope the paper is covering it."

After another pause, Sam said, "I wonder if Miss Gilmore needs some extra reporters today."

Joe glanced at Sam and David, then sprang to his feet. "What are we waiting for? Come on! Let's get over to the *Chronicle* office. Sorry, Mom, but we need to get to work on this story right away!"

"But wait a minute," Ellen protested. "You haven't even started your break——"

It was too late. The three kids had already bolted out the kitchen door.

Wishbone looked longingly at the delicious food waiting on the counter. "Ellen, don't do anything with that food until we get back. I know it's not like me to run away from vittles, and, believe me, it pains me to do it. But . . . well . . . hey, that's the life of a newshound!"

The dog raced out the door, chasing after yet another breaking story.

About Alexander Steele

Alexander Steele is a writer of books, plays, and screenplays for both juveniles and adults. And sometimes for dogs. He has written *Tale of the Missing Mascot, Case of the On-Line Alien,* and *Case of the Unsolved Case* for the WISHBONE Mysteries series. He has also written *Moby Dog, The Last of the Breed,* and *Huckleberry Dog* for The Adventures of Wishbone series; and *Unleashed in Space* for The SUPER Adventures of Wishbone series.

Alexander has written eighteen books for children, covering such interesting subjects as pirate treasure, snow leopards, and radio astronomy. He is now in the process of creating a new series of juvenile books. It's about . . . well, he can't reveal what it's about yet. Among Alexander's plays is the award-winning *One Glorious Afternoon,* which features Shakespeare and his fellow players at the Globe Theatre.

At the age of thirteen, Alexander was given *The Complete Sherlock Holmes* as a present. He still owns the book and considers it the finest gift he has ever received. He has read every single one of the sixty stories, many of them more than once. No doubt, Sherlock Holmes was partly responsible for Alexander's deciding to write mysteries himself. Alexander has a word of caution for anyone considering reading his or her first Sherlock Holmes-type story. Beware: Sherlock Holmes is a very habit-forming hobby!

Alexander lives in New York City, but he grew up in Dallas, Texas, where he used to be a newspaper carrier.